Compiled by
FELIX SCHRÖDINGER

HOGGRILLS END

*The Little Red Engine and
Other Trite Homilies*

authorHOUSE®

AuthorHouse™ UK
1663 Liberty Drive
Bloomington, IN 47403 USA
www.authorhouse.co.uk
Phone: 0800.197.4150

© 2018 Stilovsky and Schrodinger. All rights reserved.

No part of this book may be reproduced, stored in a retrieval system, or transmitted by any means without the written permission of the author.

This is a work of fiction. All of the characters, names, incidents, organizations, and dialogue in this novel are either the products of the author's imagination or are used fictitiously.

Published by AuthorHouse 12/18/2017

ISBN: 978-1-5462-8490-1 (sc)
ISBN: 978-1-5462-8489-5 (e)

Print information available on the last page.

Any people depicted in stock imagery provided by Thinkstock are models, and such images are being used for illustrative purposes only. Certain stock imagery © Thinkstock.

This book is printed on acid-free paper.

Because of the dynamic nature of the Internet, any web addresses or links contained in this book may have changed since publication and may no longer be valid. The views expressed in this work are solely those of the author and do not necessarily reflect the views of the publisher, and the publisher hereby disclaims any responsibility for them.

CONTENTS

A Job for Life	by Jane Peters.................. 1
The Picture of a Lifetime	by Poppy Fields............... 9
Robbing Peter	by Poppy Fields.............15
The Quarken Wakes	by Felix Schrodinger..... 23
The Italian Job	by Shirley Knott 27
Comme ci, Comme ca	by Poppy Fields.............31
A Close Shave	by Jane Peters................ 37
Very Andy	by Pyotr 41
Making a Hash of It	by Adrian Swall 43
A Time and a Place	by Jane Peters................ 53
Bangers and Mash	by Shirley Knott 59
The Karmic Hockey League	by Adrian Swall 65
Business As Usual	by Jean-Claude Duvalier 67
What's in a Name?	by Don Twurry............. 75
Coincidence	by Pyotr 79
Notes on Recent History	by Jane Peters................ 97
Monky Business	by Percy Verance.......... 117
A Nod and a Wink	by Bernadette Nunn 121
The Little Red Engine	by Pyotr 129
The Immaculate Conception	by Shirley Knott 135
The Letters	by Shirley Knott 139
The Tower of Babel	by Pyotr 143

Bird Spottin'	By Robin Twitcher	149
Points of View	by Jane Peters	153
About Time	by Felix Schrodinger	157
My Musical Friends	by Pyotr	161
Gobbolino the Witch's Cat	by Pyotr	165
Lurning Inglish	Anon	169
Blending In	by Lee Frake	171
A Suitable Case for Treatment	by Avril Enganes	177
The Road to Damascus	by Pyotr	181
Hoggrills End	by Pyotr	185
Pyotr and Jana at the Zoo	by Lee Frake	193
No Escape	Jane Peters	201
I Am a WIMP	by Pyotr	205
Last Minutes	by Percy Verance	209
Don't Let the Cat……..	by Felix Schrodinger	211
University Challenge	by Pyotr	219
Look back in……	by Pyotr	221
Unidentified	by Pyotr	225
Rules of Engagement	by Adrian Swall	229
Swoop and Squat	by Pyotr	235

FOREWORD

I had intended to write a novel with this title (Hoggrills End) but every time I got started, another theme cropped up in my mind and I just had to get it onto paper. So, no novel, just a collection of short stories on a (very) wide range of subjects with some adult language and themes thrown in. Some of the stories may be unsuitable for those of tender years so you might just check for me that the publishers have placed a 'PG18' note on the cover.

I chose to allow Felix to 'compile' the stories as he has a better stage presence than me but, being a cat, he has obviously not written the personal stories which form a part of the content. They were produced over a period of at least twenty years so some have to be read in the context of the time when they were written.

Unlike most anthologies, these stories are very different from each other, and you may wish, therefore, to take a short break after finishing one and before starting another. If just one of them provides you with cause for reflection or a lasting memory, then I will have achieved more than most.

With the exception of my personal recollections, which are clearly denoted, this is a work of fiction. Names, characters, businesses, places, events and incidents are either the products of my imagination or used in a fictitious manner. Any resemblance to actual persons, living or dead, or actual events is purely coincidental.

My right to be identified as author of this work has been asserted in accordance with The Copyright, Designs and Patents Act of 1988.

Pyotr Stilovsky
December 2017

A JOB FOR LIFE   BY JANE PETERS

PROLOGUE

Fatima was at her wits' end. The latest girl had performed well and he had expressed his delight by giving her an expensive diamond pendent to wear just above her mons pubis. This was just as if he had given the pendent to Fatima herself and she had congratulated herself that his trips to Singapore would be a thing of the past.

But now, just a few weeks later he had informed her that he would be travelling alone to Bangkok on the eighth and would not be back until the fifteenth. He might just stop off in Singapore for some shopping. This was too long for him to go without, as Fatima knew, but too short a time to pick up a new wife - she knew him well.

When they met she had been Donna; he had picked her up managing a small bordello in New Orleans, had been struck by her businesslike approach, and had offered her the job of *Number One Wife* in his harem just a week after meeting her.

"I can't do that," she'd said, but he'd persuaded her that it was a managerial post like any other and the Head of the Harem was not herself required to undertake conjugal duties. She accepted on condition that he paid her American taxes, kept up her health scheme contributions, bought her a private pension and allowed her to buy those-things-Americans-cannot-do-without from the JC Penny catalog.

"I'll buy you a whole hospital and an insurance company," he said "if that's what you want." But she decided that was over the top, as it wasn't a job for life, and went to work for him almost immediately. It was three years before she realised that she had a problem and had thought that she had solved it - that is until he announced his latest trip.

Jason was a nice boy by anybody's reckoning and he was in the process of making himself even nicer when the call came. He was experimenting with a fine kohl lining above his luscious lashes. He liked the way that the natural colourant enhanced his own natural dark colouring and dark brown eyes.

"Smithers, the CE wants you and I reckon your arse is on the carpet," was the gist, "and clean that bloody lipstick off before you go in - you know it makes him mad."

Jason complied though he could not see how his lipstick and false nails was relevant to the job at hand - after all his friends at the radio studio all wore it and no one complained at them. "I'll join the Beeb in my next life," he vowed.

When he entered the holy shrine of the CE's office he knew that it was serious and prepared for the worst. It was even worse. Instead of being fired the CE put a comforting arm round him and told him that he had been assigned to cover The Emirate for the magazine for the next six months.

"Just a temporary thing while Hancock recovers from his shrapnel wounds," he said, "and it will be good experience for your next job - wherever that is - remember we're not in the *job's for life* game."

When he picked up his ticket from the travel desk Jason noticed, with some misgivings, that it was a one-way ticket.

The Emirate was one of those small places that consist of sand, oil wells, Rollers and terrorists - and the Magazine had its Eastern headquarters there as the rent was incredibly cheap and they could sell copy to the wires every time there was an incident.

He soon settled down and found that he fitted in well with the cosmopolitan society. No one bothered if he came to work in high heels or dyed his hair and soon he had grown it into a fashionable bob having it set every two weeks by a hairdresser who was completely in tune with his tastes. Unfortunately the hairdresser was also in tune with one of those acronyms that abound in the Middle East (or West Asia as it is sometimes known) and earmarked our Jason as an easy target for kidnapping.

"He's a respected journalist for one of the top English Newspapers," he'd said, repeating what Jason had told him, parrot fashion, "and that will get you a lot of publicity in the UK."

So, Jason was 'taken' one quiet Sunday morning from his flat and bundled into the boot of a battered Mercedes. They had been quite friendly to him as he did not resist and allowed him to take some belongings. He was a little miffed at having to leave behind the little black number that he had bought in Dubai but they didn't seem to understand that it was his.

For a month they kept him in one room of a secure house that was so close to the Palace that no one would suspect its use. Since he never complained or tried to escape he soon built up a rapport with his captors. Neither the Mag nor the Foreign Office seemed concerned about his loss and, since there was no one at home to keep his name in the papers, they soon forgot about this other hostage.

His captors found that they had a problem. They didn't want to dispose of him as they still felt that he would pay off in the long term but they couldn't afford the manpower to keep him in solitary isolation for any longer. They would have to move him to the same location as the other hostages where he could be kept secure along with them. It was sticky-back tape time.

Jason blew his top when they explained the procedure for moving him to the prison house on the other side of the City which involved him being swathed in tape from head to foot before being bundled into the boot of the battered Mercedes and driven across the city.

"We have to do it that way to avoid you being seen by the security forces," they said, though they virtually trusted him not to escape.

"Please don't do it," he pleaded "I'm claustrophobic and I'll die." and then he had a brainwave. "Suppose I can suggest a way that will enable you to move me without risk of recognition, will you do it?"

After some consideration they agreed and asked what his plan was.

"Simple," he explained "you will dress me as an Arab woman, complete with nicab and you can take me across the city in broad daylight without any risk of discovery."

They conferred and instead of referring to higher authority decided to accept his scheme as it was neat and got rid of the problem without further night work that they were all sick of.

They brought him the clothes of an Arab woman which were supposedly discards from the Emir's harem. They also gave him his makeup bag so that he could apply a tan and some light toning to emphasise his feminine aspects. He asked for some padding and underwear and fashioned a female shape though under the flowing black garb he could have been a weightlifter and no one would have known.

Came the time to depart and he was bustled out into the street, dressed in his chosen attire and blinking at the sunlight. They would have to traverse the length of the narrow cobbled street alongside the Emir's Palace to get to the main thoroughfare where the Mercedes was parked and waiting. As they walked casually along, with a captor on each side of him, the side door of the Palace opened and from the other end of the street a black clad crocodile swung into view and proceeded toward them. His captors bustled him to the side of the street away from the door and linked their arms through his. They indicated that he was to be still and quiet.

The crocodile was escorted by six burly eunuchs, each equipped with a large baseball bat and at the rear were two palace guards with M16 rifles.

"Turn away." called the leading eunuch "It is an offence to look upon His Highness' Harem."

Jason's captors turned obediently to the wall, the three of them still with linked arms, and held him up against it between them. He looked down and from the corner of his eye could judge the progress of the procession as it passed them. One of the Eunuchs positioned himself immediately behind with his back to them, facing towards the crocodile and the side door of the Palace.

Jason judged his moment to perfection. As the crocodile was halfway into the Palace door he put all his weight onto his arms, lifted his legs in front of him and kicked out hard against the wall with both feet. All three of them went over backwards, taking the unsuspecting guard with them. As the eunuch went over in a string of curses, the rear end of the crocodile collapsed onto him. Jason was down groveling on the floor and wailing in amongst the Emir's wives before his captors were aware of what was happening. Within seconds the rest of the eunuchs were wading in with their bats to separate the men from the women, beating Jason's captors in the process.

Jason attempted to join the crocodile as it reformed but one of his captors jumped up to restrain him, shouting to the guards in Arabic - presumably that Jason was an impostor rather than a concubine. The chief eunuch strolled over and looked carefully into Jason's face. He looked into his wonderful brown eyes with its exquisite kohl liner and turned back to Jason's captors. "Don't be ridiculous." he waved them aside and "Get inside!" to Jason.

Jason meekly entered the side door of the palace. That was the last that his captors saw of him. In fact no one outside of the Palace ever saw him again.

EPILOGUE

Fatima congratulated herself on her good fortune and her perception in seeing, at once, the value of her new find. As a 'walk-in' off the street, it had been even easier than ordering a frying pan from Penny's.

The Emir never bothered again with his trips to Singapore and they all lived happily ever after.

THE PICTURE OF A LIFETIME BY POPPY FIELDS

Albert took up photography when he borrowed a camera to take some slides of the process at his place of work. Not often were the operators invited to give a talk about their work - the managers always kept this for themselves - but not now. He bought six rolls of film out of petty cash and, by the time his results came back from the developer, he was hooked. The clincher was the ease of using an automatic camera - no 'f' this or that and worrying about the film speed. You just pop the film in the back of the camera and take it out when it's finished.

He decided to join the company's photographic club and started to enter the competitions. But this was where he found that his talents were limited. He had a reasonable eye for composition and colour and was recognised as the guy to set up the group photo that went in the club magazine each year. This involved his specialty in using the delayed timer on his Pentax so that he could get into the shot himself. There was always much jocularity on these occasions and Albert enjoyed the attention. But he always seemed to just miss the moment or the angle when the result would have been a winner. Religiously he entered every club competition for the next five years and achieved a commended third on two occasions.

Instead of limiting his ambition he was fired up by the idea that he was pursuing too narrow a path to succeed and set out to broaden his horizons. He rapidly fired off a batch of entries to the Midland Group exhibitions and was not the least put off by their immediate return, complete with firm but constructive rejections. He decided that his face was not well enough known and that he would have to join the establishment.

So, he volunteered to go along as representative to Midlands meetings of the Federation to which the club was affiliated. Boredom rapidly set in as they all talked about agendas and arrangements for judging and exhibitions. No one mentioned photography - ever! He passed it on to someone else after a year realising it was not the route to success.

"I wouldn't mind but all I want is a really good picture that everyone will admire - and if it got published that would be the ultimate for me." he bewailed to his wife Sonia.

But she was more concerned about the expense of his hobby and how it ate into their nest egg for retirement. "You must have taken eight films last week and how much has that cost?" she responded.

"It'll pay for itself if I sell some," he said "one of the guys in the club won two hundred quid in a comp last week."

"Not you though," she said. "You spend a fortune on that bloody camera and we don't even get a good picture of the cat to frame."

He had a problem focusing on dark fur and they were always a bit blurred. He sought solace in cleaning his lenses with the squirrel-hair brush she had bought him at Christmas.

Back at the club he sought advice and, instead of realising his limitations, ended up buying a new wide angle lens from the club know-all who assured him that his shots would never again be out of focus. With this Albert and his long suffering spouse set off on their annual pilgrimage to the north of Scotland.

"Let's go and see the seals off the headland," she suggested after two days of comparative boredom, hedged in by the rain and the midges. "At least the mozzies won't be there and you can go along and photograph the gannets if it's not too windy."

She hated to make these suggestions as it usually resulted in him using two rolls of film instead of one and the outcome would be thirty identical pictures of minute birds in the distance.

"Need a longer lens." he complained, but it never stopped him shooting off another roll.

They left the Reliant Robin at the official car park and walked the three miles along the narrow cliff top road glowering at the other tourists who ignored the prohibition and drove all the way out to the headland. They took tea and scones at the small tea-room at the lighthouse and suitably refreshed set out to spot the seals which would surface off the headland. It was a strange phenomenon. The seal watchers clustered in small groups, resplendent in yellow and orange waterproofs, out on the sloping pink rocks. And the seals gathered about fifty meters out in the swell and looked at the watchers. You could easily imagine the seals discussing their arrangements for the day and deciding to go to the headland for a morning's people watching.

After half an hour they tired of the seals and he decided to take the cliff path to the gannet sanctuary. She decided it was too windy and did not have the right shoes on. Do women ever have the right shoes on? Albert set off accompanied only by his trusty Pentax.

As he went along the cliff side path he took great care as the path often sloped at forty five degrees down to the edge and there was a stiff breeze blowing. He had always been aware that you had to be the early worm, or boldly go, to get the photograph that would turn out to be a winner. As he came to the outcrop alongside the colony he realised that he had left his longer lens on the back seat of the car - he only had the wide angle lens on the camera and that was no good for the gannets, forty or fifty meters away across the water on a rocky outlier. Behind him the gulls wheeled and soared in the wind.

"Must get a picky." he muttered to himself, after investing a mile of clambering along the side of the cliffs on a very difficult path; he was not going back empty handed. He decided to use the cliff and the soaring gulls as a background and take a delayed shot with himself in the foreground. So long as he kept the shutter setting right his new wide angle lens would keep everything in focus. He could just see it on the wall in the club and everyone admiring it. "What setting did you use Albert?" "Is it on Maxfax 200 or did you try the Fujifuzz 25?" they would say.

He carefully selected his site where the cliff went down vertically from the outcrop in order to get the maximum impact but was careful not to take risks. He put the camera on the auto-timer setting and selected an almost level turf that allowed him to angle the camera upwards. Of course he couldn't get behind the camera to check his composition as there was only the vertical drop to the rocks behind it. Satisfied that all was well he selected a tump about five feet from the camera and sat on it. Then he looked behind and checked the sky and the wheeling seabirds. Everything was right. He leaned carefully across to the camera and pressed the shutter release. As expected nothing happened except the little red light began to flash slowly. It would do this for seven seconds then flash quickly for another three before opening the shutter to take the photo.

Albert counted the seconds but suddenly realised that he had not put the cover onto the eyepiece to shield out the light. He reached out for the camera to stop it and at that moment the wind gusted. As he grasped it, he took off like a hang glider from a cliff face and as the wind took him over the cliff he dropped the camera. They fell together, separated by a meter or two, under the influence of gravity for no more than two seconds when the shutter was opened for a split second and then closed again.

After his cremation the club members gathered to see Albert's last photo. It was a masterpiece, and a conundrum that no one could figure out, showing Albert flying in mid air and the gannet colony all in perfect focus. It was the picture of a lifetime.

Sonia sold it to a tabloid newspaper and retired to the West Country on the proceeds. She said she never had the right shoes for Scotland.

ROBBING PETER — BY POPPY FIELDS

"It's all a matter of personality," the speaker was saying "not of technical skills."

Paul was listening to Dr Marten, current guru of the management world and author of *The Reverse Peter Principle*. It was the use of the name in the title that had first brought the auspicious Doctor to his attention - prior to that he had thought that the guru was a boot manufacturer from Northampton.

"Of course everyone is familiar with the *Peter Principle* - that employees in an organisation rise to their level of incompetence i.e. one level above competence; and that this is due to managements', or the individual's, inability to recognise that doing your current job well can be satisfying and rewarding to many people. Not everyone needs advancement."

"My *Reverse Peter Principle* - the RPP - is much more useful but demands greater effort on the part of management to recognise the situation. It is based on the premise that potential managers are bored by the more lowly tasks and do not do them well. Thus, in extremis, a high flier will make a botch of the budget form because he has no interest in that level of detail and will not listen to the clerk who is expert at that level. The clerk is thus amazed that such an ignoramus should be promoted when he can't even do the simplest tasks."

"Once on the ladder the subject of our principle soon realises that doing the job yourself is a mug's game and there are plenty of lemmings out there. The allocation, or buying in, of resources soon becomes the only way to proceed with a task - for our 'man' (if you will permit me to be sexist in my terminology) is not a doer himself."

"At each promotion he will improve as each time he raises his level in the organisation he has access to a greater range of support and external services. This is why we tend to find that our great managers are not made from the academic achievers of our college days but from the team captains and even the bullies who had ways - good or bad - of persuading others to do the mundane tasks for them. They also seek sponsorship from those who have already succeeded and later return it to others who would themselves succeed but are further down the ladder."

"My purpose is not to decry the role of the technocrat, the specialist and the administrator - but simply to put them into context. Promote not the man who has just shown his adequacy in his current post but the bored underachiever who aspires to lead - help show him the way."

"Thank you and goodnight."

The presentation closed to rapturous applause and as Paul filed out with the other 'suits' who had packed the seminar he was surprised to see an old friend from his previous employment. They had worked together for two or three years before James had moved on to better things. They greeted each other like the long lost friends they were and retired to the bar for a few drinks before going home.

As they went over their experiences since their last meeting Paul became aware that James had subtly changed. He was a more rounded person and was inclined to see the bigger picture. His personal life had not, however, reflected his advancement on the business scene. He was in the throes of divorce though, to all accounts, not a bitter one. His wife felt that he was not the gentle, caring person she had married and she no longer wished to be part of his life.

That said, he had achieved much in the time since they had last seen each other, being vice-president of a software development company. Paul soon started to compare his own progress.

"You heard what Dr Marten was saying about the 'RPP'? Well that's how I see things but I'm on the wrong end of it - instead of looking down the telescope at my great future it's as if I'm looking at the other end and I'm going to vanish into obscurity. Whenever I ask for more resources they tell me to do it myself and then congratulate me on a good job."

"It's the same with Peter - you know - from the computer department we're complete opposites but we both get the same treatment. He's lively and a natural talker and people love to be around him but he lacks my tact and diplomacy so people get upset when he steps out of line. People say we should be shaken up together in a bag."

James apologised that he would have to leave but gave Paul his own business card and that of another organisation. The other card read:

EGO INCORPORATED
Make the best of your personality
Toll free 0365-66-666

Paul was intrigued and at first thought that, because of the 6's in the number that he was being propositioned to sell his soul. James assured him that it was not like that and suggested he make contact with them as soon as he could.

"They worked wonders for me," was his parting shot.

The next morning he was on the phone booking an appointment for his first consultation and picked up a cancellation at short notice. On entering the building he was struck by the sheer size of the organisation and the opulence of the decor. "Nothing cheap here," he thought, "just the smell of success."

He met a quiet man, who he took for a psychologist and a lady who gave him a number of psychometric tests - the sort you get on a management assessment but much less obscure. Inside three hours he had told them who he was and what he wanted and had poured out his heart over his lack of progress. They appeared impressed with his resolve and acquainted him with the fee scale for their services.

"This is a total package - you can't just take part of it - and it has to be geared to the availability of the required components. It's a bit like replacement organ surgery and there's no point trying to do a heart transplant if you don't have a donor." They explained that finding donors was not all that difficult as you could buy anything but where a mutual exchange could be arranged that was even better.

He agreed that he wished to proceed and signed up to the payment schedule which amounted to almost $1m over the next ten years. At this point their attention switched to the mention he had made of his colleague and the qualities that Peter had that would enhance Paul's personality and vice versa. At the end of the session Paul was counseled to get Peter along to see if he wanted to join the programme.

To Paul's surprise Peter was almost immediately persuaded and went for his first session within the next week. As he had difficulties on the financial front - they offered Peter a free lower grade service provided he kept all his appointments and made himself available for training purposes. Paul overlooked the discrepancy with what they had offered him.

Everything was going fine and the counselors laid out a personality profile that would be bound to ensure his success. They told him that Peter's progress was a little problematical and would require more time so they should not compare notes. At this point the alarm bells rang and he realised that they were setting up to transfer to him those attributes that he desired from his own colleague. After the initial panic and wavering he rationalised that life wasn't fair and he had been robbed of a share of his rightful attributes at birth. He said nothing.

On the fateful day of his transfer Paul recorded with disinterest that Peter also had an appointment that day and geared himself up for the greatest moment of his life. The transfer took over two hours during which time he was largely unconscious of what was happening but at the end he certainly felt different.

"Go home and take the next few days to acclimatise. Don't be surprised if you want to do new things or if you respond in a different way from predicted. That's all part of the settling in process. Don't touch any alcohol or drugs for at least ten days. Go to work as normal next week and just watch out for the difference. Call if you have any problems."

With this and best wishes for his new future he left the offices of EGO INCORPORATED and stepped out into his brave new world.

He followed all of the instructions and returned to work as a new man. At first this paid off and he made great strides in his projects and succeeded where previously he might have failed. He applied for a new post and was rewarded with an immediate interview, narrowly missing the job which was given to an ex Olympic swimmer. "EI couldn't have transferred that across," he consoled himself and prepared himself for his next leap.

However this was taken over by events as his application had brought him to the attention of the senior VP for the area. His file was reviewed and shortly he was asked to retake all of the personality profile tests that he had done on his management assessment. His results were reviewed by the head of Human Resources and the VP and their judgment was clear.

"He's changed completely from the guy we had last year - he's lost most of the basic qualities that have made him so useful. He has to go."

And so Paul was 'delayered' in a departmental reorganisation and was sent out to join all of the other souls who had been 're-engineered', 'downsized', 'undeployed', 'redundized' and those who had just been sacked.

His sense of outrage was justified and he took out his contract from EGO INCORPORATED to see what redress he had. No satisfaction was guaranteed - not even a partial recovery. Despite this he made an appointment as they had told him to do in the event of trouble and the following day he met the psychologist who had briefed him.

To Paul's surprise he was most understanding and after a phone call to their quality control department agreed to refund all of his fees and cancel their agreement. Paul shook hands and left with a sense of relief.

As he walked through the expensive marble foyer and approached the priceless stained glass revolving door he noticed a Cadillac limousine from which emerged a dapper Armani clad man of his own age and build. As Peter came in through the door the concierge saluted.

"Peter," called Paul "how are you?"

"Why Hello Paul," said Peter, greeting him and taking him by the arm in that way that great men do with their underlings.

"I'm fine. Remember last month that I came in for a minor training session - you know, the day you came for treatment. Well after the training session I ended up being interviewed for the post of Marketing President and I got it. They said I have the perfect personality for the job."

THE QUARKEN WAKES BY FELIX SCHRODINGER

"Professor Starling, we're ready when you are," called the techie. "It's all set on line two and Johnson is asking if you'll look in on this one, we're completely stumped."

"I'll be there in ten." he responded polite as he ever was, but not a man to waste words. To waste them would distract from his thinking time and that might mean that that his time on earth was reduced by that exquisite fraction that meant he would not achieve his goal.

Ever since his schooldays he had been like this when his interest had been awoken in science, not by the tedium of the chemistry or physics lab, but by the great British science fiction writer John Wyndham. He had read and reread *The Day of the Triffids* but his favourite remained, as always, *The Kraken Wakes*. The anti-matter particle, which was the subject of his life's work, had been named the *Quarken* as a sort of pun between its parent opposite - the *Quark* - and Wyndham's *Kraken*.

And now it was in sight - literally. The new particle analyser could pick up the traces resulting from the collisions that were produced at the end of the accelerator and turn out a computer generated image that was better than anything the Americans or CERN could produce. The unraveling of the nature of anti-matter was just a matter of time.

Starling's success at Cambridge had come, not from following scientific method but from the source of all great scientific discoveries - inspiration and intuition - a realisation that here or there was a new possibility that had not yet occurred to anyone else. He based his ethos on a quaint mixture of eastern and western philosophies, having been greatly influenced by Oppenheimer and the Los Alamos project. Oppenheimer had named the first bomb *Trinity* after the Hindu Gods: Brahma, Vishnu and Shiva. Starling thought the choice significant and had wondered why Oppenheimer had not gone simply for Shiva - the Destroyer. His researches had taken him into eastern philosophies and the result was a blend of science and occult that no one but he recognised or acknowledged.

All of his major advances had come during sleep, meditation or out of the blue - you know that feeling you get - "I wonder where that came from?" Starling had long given up on his colleagues in the physiological and psychological sciences who continued to insist that they would soon unlock the secrets of the brain. His argument was that it was simply the receiver of messages and controller of the physical body.

Unable to get time on the CERN accelerator he looked for alternatives and just as the personal computer had revolutionised its field he had produced a particle accelerator that would fit in a lab instead of underneath a whole mountain. The concept was elegant and simple and it revolutionised particle physics as every physics department, with $2m to spare, could own one. The accelerator itself was cheap but the devices that they used to record the particle tracks had not kept pace and they were now developing this alongside their original research into the *Quarken*.

Today, as they had done every day for the last ten weeks, they would accelerate a charged particle to within a fraction of light speed and crash it into a target particle suspended in a magnetic fluid. As the particles broke, fleeting glances of their constituents could be caught on photographic film - at least that was the way it had been done. The trouble with film was that it was two dimensional and this was where Starling had aimed his next major advance. The nature of the *Quarken* would be his as soon as he had the new three-dimensional analyser working and correlated. But first they had to solve this little bug that the techie had discovered.

The apparatus was based on holding the target particle in a magnetic field which was steady and continuously recorded in three dimensions by remote devices that did not themselves disturb the field. When the accelerated particle hit the target the changes in the magnetic field were recorded and this was used to track the resulting particles. The computer-enhanced results were providing a new look at the meaning of matter - or at least one small piece of it - the *Quarken*.

The lab technician and his assistant sat beside the optical viewer which was the only opening into the collision chamber. This was used to set up the physical components before each test. Like a laser the whole operation used only low power and it was possible to watch the collision through the porthole eyepiece. From the size and colour of the minute impact you got a feel for the quality of the run.

They decided to run the experiment and Starling would add his observations to his assistants' to see if they could iron out the bug before going home. The problem was the normal particles were not tracking where they should and this was making it difficult to pick out the *Quarken* from the background.

"I've tried a new setting on the target angle and we appear to have lost the particle completely," said the assistant, "neither of us can see it on the analysis afterwards. Perhaps you could look?"

Starling put his eye to the eyepiece; fine tuned the focus and then gently pressed the start button. The emitter came to life and, within seconds, the accelerator warmed up, the green light came on and he initiated the fire sequence. He saw a small orange flash within the target area and the particles split as expected. However, instead of the *Quarken* streaking out beyond the target area it shot at right angles into the eyepiece, through the optics, through Starling's eyeball and into his skull where the soft spongy tissue of his brain halted its progress and his great mind absorbed its full impact.

"I just had a thought." he said, turning to his colleagues.

THE ITALIAN JOB BY SHIRLEY KNOTT

"I don't suppose he ever came here because you just see the cars go into the tunnel entrance and then after the underground sequence they're back in Turin. They would have been driven by stunt men rather than Michael and his mates. But the sequence inside the tunnel was definitely here - it was in the Sowe Valley sewer. They'd finished building it and used it for filming before they turned the sewage into it. Best film ever made." he said as if to sum it up.

"What was?" queried Elliot, the chief salesman coming into the conversation halfway through.

"You wouldn't remember." responded Fred trying to get out of going through it all again.

"Oh yes I do." said Elliot, "It was on last week and I was only asking because we've got a group of buyers over here from the Italian Army looking to buy half track Saracens for a new rapid response force."

"Going to invade Ethiopia again are they?" rejoined Fred who was noted as the department wit as well as stalwart of the sales office, "OK, when do we hit them?"

"They'll be here all week and I have to nanny them," rejoined Elliot. "I suppose it will be the Transport Museum, Warwick Castle and Stratford. Do you think you could do the castle – I've been there fifteen times and it's beginning to pall."

"I'll do it for you," replied Fred, "so long as none of them surrender to the suits of armour - but who's doing the tech spec?"

"You, as far as I know," replied Elliot "so no more jokes about the *Italian Book of War Heroes* or we may lose the order."

As predicted the Italians stayed for the week and were most impressed with the light tank. They were shown the construction, the cadmium corrosion protection, the component suppliers and the vehicle assembly. Each of them had his own specialty so Enrico looked at the gun and went to the firing range; Federico was engaged with the chassis and the bodywork. Giorgio, the leader was an engine and transmission specialist. He spent hours watching the Daimler engine being put together and was enthralled with the gearbox assembly. Not only did he write everything down but he meticulously repeated it all back to check his facts.

"So the engine is a supercharged four and a half litre petrol unit that runs on standard leaded fuel - when will you convert to unleaded?"

"Let me confirm - the tank has seven forward gears and two reverse and you are offering it with a manual gearbox - the Americans are using automatics - when do you plan to change?"

"The driving position is at the front below the con and this restricts the driver's rear view - how does he see to reverse?"

This and many others were answered all to the apparent satisfaction of the delegation and at the end of the week the deal seemed set for a satisfactory conclusion. At that point Giorgio made contact with his Minister at home and confirmed the pertinent details; going through, in great detail, the performance, the engine options, transmission, armament and many others facets.

"Yes the fire control system is better than the French one.......yes seven forward and two reverse......four and a half litres......50 mm with armour piercing......." Thus he went on into the night and the following morning, after a long session with Enrico and only two hours sleep he called Elliot to say that they were ready for the final session.

"Your price is fine and we like almost everything about the tank - it's ideal for our purpose of rapid response but the Minister has asked me to make one major change to your standard specification and then the deal can be signed."

Giorgio continued hesitantly and listed all of the things they were satisfied with until Elliot, who had also been up most of the night, began to tire. Eventually he confronted Giorgio and addressed him directly.

"Yes but what is that you want changed?"

"Well... actually...." stuttered Giorgio.... "we want you to put the body on the other way round."

COMME CI, COMME CA BY POPPY FIELDS

Fothergill knew there would be trouble on his return and sure enough the tabloids were there at the airport, baying at him like hyenas round a wounded animal. There's nothing like the Press when they smell a wounded politician - especially on the return trip from an EC meeting in France.

He was dreading having to make his report to Smithers at Number 10 as it appeared that the Frogs had done it again. That dreadful de Grenouilles at the Quai D'Orsay had backed him into a corner and had then switched agendas. He had not seen it coming and had conceded major ground on the currency before realising that he should have consulted first. He would be lucky to survive the week despite Smithers' confidence statement. He desperately needed to confer with Hardwick before he was called in to the office and was greatly relieved to find the Transport Minister waiting for him in the hall at Number 10.

Fortunately the PM was otherwise engaged with lobbyists concerned with the new gun controls.

"That should give us at least twenty minutes to plan an escape route." thought Fothergill.

He was greatly relieved to find that Hardwick was already aware of his difficulties and had even warned against his planned meeting with de Grenouilles. Now he had a plan to rescue his friend from utter humiliation. Hardwick outlined his strategy and Fothergill at once saw the route to saving his ministerial salary and chauffeur driven car. When the PM was free they entered the inner office with an air of confidence.

"Don't worry about the EC," pre-empted Hardwick, "we have bigger fish to fry and after we've finished de Grenouilles won't even be in the government."

Smithers was taken aback at the strength of the Transport Minister's charge and retreated behind his desk. After all, he had recently addressed the old enemy in their own language and he had a liking for holidays across the little stretch of water that separated the old Normans from the new.

Hardwick continued as soon as he had caught breath.

"You remember the great debate about the line that the Channel Rail Link was to take into London - and how all parties favoured the cheaper, southern route into Waterloo?"

"Yes," replied the bemused PM, "but what has that to do with the EC and Toad (their nickname for de Grenouilles)?"

"Well," continued Hardwick, "it appears that Toad, in his previous job as my equivalent in transport, was given a top priority job by his government. He was to use all means at his disposal to ensure that Frenchmen would no longer have to suffer the indignity of arriving at a station named after their greatest defeat ever on land. He did everything possible to sabotage the southern route to Waterloo and they even bought small parcels of land all along the proposed track. He gave these, under a cover, to the protest groups opposing that route!"

"When his campaign was successful and we chose the northern route to St Pancras he was promoted into the Chancellor's job within weeks and he's been on top of the pile ever since - don't you see - if we reverse our decision over the link and go back to Waterloo, he'll be discredited and we'll not have to stick to yesterday's agreement."

Smithers was intrigued but not persuaded - millions had been spent on buying land along the northern route, the designs were finalised and the financing package (give or take a few hiccups) was again in place. Reverting to the old route at this late stage - even with good reason - would seriously affect the government's credibility. Though Fothergill and Hardwick could not see it, the damage could be just as bad as the EC fiasco.

The time was rapidly approaching when the returnee was due to address a packed House of Commons and they were still locked in the dilemma when Hardwick had an insight so brilliant - they agreed that this would be his finest hour. They left immediately for the house convinced that he had saved the day.

The PM gave his usual drubbing to the leader of the opposition whose questions consisted of carefully baited traps and rarely contained substance. If he'd known that most of them were sent over, and often set, by his mole in the party, he could have improved his performance overnight - but he didn't and so the opposition languished - in interminable opposition.

After a few fruitless sorties the Shadow Chancellor rose and asked whether the PM supported his recently returned Minister on the outcome of his talks with our friends across the water in Paris.

The PM rose and espoused his support for Fothergill, to much noise from the opposition who had sensed Fothergill's blood. He then surprised the House by telling them that there were greater things afoot and the Minister of Transport would make a statement. The house hummed at this unexpected turn of events.

Hardwick was not a great orator but in the thirty minutes since they had left Number 10, he and Fothergill had put together a short but telling indictment of the plotters who had hatched such a diabolical scheme against the sovereign state of Albion.

He exposed the scope of his investigations, laid down the facts and told the house that a statement supporting them would be placed in the library the following morning. The members were agog that such perfidious behavior should come from a neighbouring ally and listened intently to as he delivered every measured word.

Having given out the facts, and identified the culprits, he came to the final sentence which they had carefully crafted.

"I have, therefore, to inform the house that, on the 21st of October, 2001, when Her Majesty declares the new link open, that the ceremony will take place at the restored St Pancras Station which will, from that day forth, be known as Trafalgar!"

Hardwick sat down to rapturous applause from both sides of the house and Fothergill's day was saved.

De Grenouilles resigned the next day.

A CLOSE SHAVE BY JANE PETERS

Bill had been hitting the bottle for a while; it wasn't the problems with his marriage, it was just the boring work situation and the lack of other things to do. There are only so many restaurants that you can eat in a foreign city and if you don't like the company there's not much else to do.

He always argued that there were only two kinds of people who worked overseas - those who went to get away from the problems at home, and those who got problems at home because they worked abroad. Bill had started off in the first camp and rapidly progressed to the second so he had the worst of both worlds. He followed a well worn ex-pat path that involved consuming a bottle of spirits nearly every day.

One of the problems with alcohol abuse is loss of appetite and Bill was no exception so he skipped breakfast, tucked in to egg and chips at lunchtime and had a bottle of Bagpiper for supper. As any nutritionist will tell you this is not enough for a healthy gut and, following a nasty bout of the runs, Bill was laid low.

He had been contemplating an evening out for real food when the pain hit him. He was doubled up in agony and had to be helped to his room by the hotel staff. After that he just couldn't stop going. When the squitters refused to go away he was referred by the hotel doctor to a bowel consultant at the local hospital. He was soon diagnosed as having a lesion in his bowel. He had been due to travel home, but could not keep to a sitting position long enough to make the flight, so he was brought in to the hospital for an operation.

On the evening before, he was carefully supervised by Matron and a rather nice little nurse from Karnataka. Some say they are the best nurses in the world. So he had to forego his usual ration and was a bit down when the surgeon called.

"Well Mr Biscuit," said the surgeon, "you have been remiss - perhaps now you'll remember to eat your wheaty bangs. Or we'll have you in here every other week!"

"Give him a good shave, Matron, and we'll see what we can do to sort out his rear end." With that he left but Bill, minus his usual prop, was a bit apprehensive about being shaved by Matron.

His fears were groundless as Matron turned to the attractive nurse and curtly ordered that Mr Biscuit be shaved forthwith in preparation for his op in the morning. Bill was considerably perked at the prospect of being shaved by 'Nursie' as he called her and awaited her return with the shaving gear with great anticipation. So he was bitterly disappointed when the door was opened by a small man in his sixties, complete with a bowl, shaving brush and a cut throat razor. The elderly male nurse painstakingly removed the hair around his private parts and from virtually the whole of his lower body above the knee. He never said a word during the whole thirty minutes that it took him and at the end Bill's bum was as smooth as a baby's.

The surgeon was most amused as he did his pre-op examination. "Who shaved his pubes?" he questioned Matron, "we're doing his arse not his dick!" Matron flushed and said nothing - the message had probably lost a little in its passage having been received with the customary rolling of the head which can mean anything from 'OK to 'get stuffed'.

Bill was past caring anyway having had a couple of valium tablets as pre-op relaxation and was even considering giving up booze in its favour until he discovered that pentothal was even better. Certainly he was well away for the duration and the next thing he knew, after the wonderful erotic dream he had under the drug's influence, was the usual face tapping and requests from the anesthetist to wake up. This he did with some reluctance and was shipped off to the recovery ward with Nursie.

Being on a liquid diet and full of packing from the op he had no obvious problems for the next few days - other than the lack of his beloved Bagpiper – a sort of enforced cold turkey. But on the morning of the fifth day he started to get the feeling that he needed to go - not for a pee but the other thing. He called for Matron and reminded her that the surgeon was due and would he please come at the beginning of the round as the urge to go was getting quite strong.

The surgeon had still not appeared by six pm and Bill was getting frantic. He was desperate for a number two but his rectum was still full of packing from the operation. What could he do? In the end the problem resolved itself. In an explosion that could have been recorded on the Richter scale he discharged his packing thus relieved himself of the pressure build-up of the last twelve hours. He pulled the emergency cord before collapsing gently to the floor.

"Oh Mr Biscuit, you have made a mess." cried Matron, "Get yourself into the shower while we clean up.

Bill struggled into the shower and reached for the control. As he did so he felt another wave of faintness come over him and he started to fall. Grasping the shower control to slow his slide into oblivion the whole assembly came away from the wall and the open pipe showered water everywhere.

"My God, Mr Biscuit, what have you done now?" screamed Matron hauling him out of the deluge. "Nurse - call for the plumber at once."

Bill's last memory of the fiasco, before he passed out completely was the entrance of the plumber in his dark blue overalls, carrying his toolkit and a large spanner in his hand.

It was the elderly guy who had shaved him.

VERY ANDY   BY PYOTR

When I was a little lad, my Dad asked me how many times I could repeat the same word in a sensible sentence. I was quite dumfounded when he expostulated that you could use the same word five times.

He explained how a publican had asked for a new sign for his pub - **The Pig and Whistle**. He set out a draft design and the signwriter went away to make a mock-up. When it came back he looked at the sign and made some amendments.

"Look, I want more space between **Pig and 'and'** / **and 'and'**/ **and Whistle**," he said. So he wrote it down in his beautiful copperplate script and gave it to a young lady to type (no WP in those days). His writing was wonderful but, like so many that are ultra neat, it was a little difficult to read. Anyway, she typed it and handed him the draft back for checking.

"I'm not completely clear how you wanted it laid out", she said, "personally I thought you should have put an extra space between '**Pig and 'and'**"/ *and* **'and 'and'**"/ *and* **'and 'and'**"/ *and* **'and Whistle'**."

When he wrote what she had told him he realised that they had increased the original number of 'ands' from five to ten.

41

He thanked her profusely and sent it off to the conundrum section of the local newspaper for publication.

A week later a reply came under the heading of the editor of the *Andover Gazette*, our local rag.

Dear Bill (that was his name)

Many thanks for the little story which we may be able to use, but I want to take issue with you over the clarity of the piece and the use of punctuation. It looks very messy and my typesetter thinks we could usefully use some commas to make it easier to read. I propose to place them between:

Pig and 'and" and *and* **'and 'and"** and *and* **'and 'and"** and *and* **'and 'and"** and *and* **'and 'and"** and *and* **'and Whistle' ".**

This would certainly be publishable if you could get the *Guinness Book of World Records* to authenticate it. What do you think?

    Yours Sincerely

    Andrew Anders, Editor in Chief

He wrote back some two weeks later; this was his response:

Dear Editor

I have contacted The *GBoWR* and…………..

MAKING A HASH OF IT   BY ADRIAN SWALL

With a name like James Bond Ivanovich his destiny, to become a spy, was never in doubt. It was determined by his mother, a devout Ian Fleming fan, who had spent much of her life in the foreign service of her country and, through great perseverance, passed on to her offspring a love of the English language and great fluency in it.

Thus he came, after his years of basic training, to find himself outside the embassy of his native land in the great sub continent that had long ago thrown off the shackles of empire. But in those years before the cold war collapsed, the developing countries had aligned themselves with those who offered the best deal; thus James had been posted to find out what the Bald Eagle was planning next in its continuing trysts with the Great Bear.

His controller, Ivan Turdivovich, briefed him about the country and their opponents in the *Great Game* but when he discovered his pupil's penchant for 007 he left him to find out about the local operations himself. His own predilection was more delicate being based on Michael Caine and his portrayal of Harry Palmer. Whilst he had seen *The Ipcress File* at least a dozen times his favourite film was *The Italian Job*. He often dreamed about the finale and how he would stop the gold-laden coach from toppling over the edge of the gorge.

Having inherited his mother's brains and his father's good looks James set out to capture the heart of one of Uncle Sam's secretaries at the embassy. The place was so well screened that they had given up eavesdropping and had resorted to more primitive methods of spying. He masqueraded as a gas engineer from Norway who had been abroad for many years and was advising the government on the development of a new gas field.

He met Heather at the United Nations Club one Friday evening and she was at once captivated by his good looks and easygoing ways. He seemed to have plenty of money and when he told her his name she was bowled over, joking that he must be a spy sent to discover the embassy secrets. To be on the safe side she invited him to join her on the ex-pats' Hash that Sunday.

"What is a Hash?" he asked.

"Just come in your trainers and shorts with plenty of water and you'll find out," she said.

He soon found out that a Hash involved following a paper trail laid round the countryside by a hare who would also lay false trails every so often to slow down the faster runners and allow the tortoises to catch up.

"A bit like orienteering without the forest and the map," she explained.

They ambled, jogged and walked according to the ground and admired the countryside but after a while James started to worry about the land they were crossing and the litter from the paper trail that they followed.

"Don't worry," Heather told him, "we always keep to the edges of fields and by next week there's never any paper left - it just vanishes after a few days."

He stopped worrying but was intrigued by the finely shredded paper that was being left behind in discreet little patches to mark the trail.

"Where do you get the paper he asked?"

"From the embassy," she replied "- it's what comes out of the shredder."

It was food for thought for James as they wandered back for the gathering after the run.

He soon discovered that hashing did not just involve running in the sun - it also involved winding down after with a little drinking ceremony. He had consumed two beers - not easy to get hold of here - and was ready to try his luck with Heather on the way home when everyone formed into a circle at the behest of a lady who called herself the 'Grand Mattress'.

"Welcome Hashers." she greeted them and proceeded to expose poor James as a 'virgin' for which he had to stand in the centre of the ring and tell a joke. Unfortunately he could not think of a good one and ended up with a collection of groans.

"What do you think of that?" bawled the Mattress.

"Rubbish!" they responded and he found himself holding a large silver tankard of beer.

One of the group started to waggle his right index finger in the air giving out a strange wailing call. At the end of the wail the circle started to chant.

"Down, down, why are we waiting, boring, boring, down, down, down."- until all the beer was gone and he had shaken the tankard over his shoulder to show it was empty.

Two other 'virgins' introduced themselves and after their induction the group sang:

"They are Hashers it is true

They are Hashers through and through

They are Hashers so they say.........."

As the singing came to an end the "down, down" chorus began again and they all sank another beer.

James woke with a hangover but a great feeling that he broken into the local society - despite not being capable of even trying to get away with Heather - but what's more he had great news for Major Turdivovich.

At their weekly debrief he confided in his controller that there was a possibility that the Americans were foolishly spreading their (albeit shredded) confidential waste all over the countryside.

Turdivovich was impressed by James' observation but unmoved.

"Don't you think that the great minds of the mother country have not already discovered this? - come I will show you."

They left the house where James resided and travelled out in the direction where the ex-pats' hashes were usually run. Part way they changed into a battered old Datsun which took them to a village that James had seen on the Sunday. They walked into the village and entered a low hut at the edge where the smell of water buffalo was overpowering. Once inside Turdivovich called a greeting to a peasant and soon a door and steps opened up to allow them to descend into fresh cool air.

James was amazed to find himself in something out of a sci-fi movie. Under the hovels of the village was an underground bunker with the quiet hum of machinery and air conditioning. Turdivovich explained that it was built in the underground section of an old water pumping station that had been abandoned years ago. They had sited the village on top to disguise their comings and goings.

Turdivovich took him through the centre until they reached a large room with about twenty young locals all sifting gently through large amounts of shredded paper.

"As soon as the run is over, our friends go out and retrieve every scrap they can - we pay them by the gram and very well at that!" extolled Turdivovich.

"Then they sort it and iron it gently into strips so that it's like new - now comes the clever part - instead of trying to glue it back together, every strip is scanned here in this machine and digitised into code recognisable by the computer."

He turned and gestured towards a small tower in the centre of the room with flashing lights and its own air conditioning.

"But that's a Cray"! exclaimed James, "How could we possibly afford that?"

"Don't ask," responded Turdivovich, "it's our pride and joy."

"We scan the information from every scrap of paper and the computer fits it all back together - just like new; sometimes it takes only a few minutes from getting all the data but other times it can take all day. It's just found the first half dozen header strips and everything will fall rapidly into place now - just watch."

James watched with fascination as a bank of screens in front of him started to light up with pages of information and paper started to fly out from the high speed printer attached to the Cray. In another two minutes the computer was recording 97% success and 1241 page matches forming 385 continuous documents. In these it had picked up 984 key words which were being highlighted in a printout for Turdivovich to peruse.

He glanced through each of the pages and dismissed most of them to the waste paper.

"Why are we always getting the rubbish?" he exclaimed to James, "another bloody menu for the ambassador to approve! - What do they do just eat and sleep in the bloody place?" He swore a lot when he got agitated.

"The General wants results from this set up - and all we get is crap - it cost more than a whole year's budget just for the computer and the cost of adapting the building was as much. Please go and see if you can persuade this young lady to tell you what is going wrong."

James saw Heather after the run as he did not want to get into a lather before approaching her. She was standing by a table laden with whole mangoes and she had a sharp knife in her hand.

"Hello," he said' "I thought I'd missed you."

"Cheers," she responded, "felatio or cunnilingus?"

He looked at her curiously - this was not what he expected of a young American girl - and an attractive one at that.

Testing his luck he responded "Felatio please."

She promptly picked up a large mango and deftly cut around the stone following the smaller circumference. A quick twist and the upper half was separated from the stone which remained attached to the other half. She invited him to suck the flesh from the stone and he realised why it was referred to as felatio.

"What do you do for cunnilingus?" he asked.

She picked up another mango and slit it around the long edge, separating the upper half from the stone. She then cut below the stone and removed it. She offered him the two halves from which he extracted the fruit with a spoon.

"The spoon's optional." she said.

After the hashing ceremony James dutifully approached Heather and, after a few beers, he discovered that she was only too willing to talk about the shredded confidential waste from the Embassy.

"Well," she started, "it's like this - we shred all our medium grade waste and then spread it out over the countryside every Sunday. The reason it's gone so soon is because this Russky spy called Turdivovich has the locals pick it up and then he straightens all the paper out. After that he scans every piece and then processes the results on a second hand Cray that we sold him. It was surplus from the Pentagon about five years ago and it must have soaked up most of his budget for at least two years. That means that he can't follow us around and go through the rubbish bins at the embassy like he used to do - simply because he can't afford to do it anymore."

"When he gets the print-outs most of it is useless but we feed him the odd scrap from time to time just to keep his attention. We even have the menus printed with the dishes as key words like 'F16' and 'Forrestal' so the computer will pick them out - great laugh isn't it?"

James pretended to be amused and then broached the subject of the really sensitive documents.

"Oh we never shred them," explained Heather, "there's no need - they're all printed on supersoft letter paper and after they're finished with we cut them into four and use them as toilet paper."

James was dumbfounded at the subterfuge and couldn't wait to tell Turdivovich what was happening. He was also amazed at the profligacy of the Americans who only made four sheets of toilet paper from letter sized paper - at home it would be at least six!

At their next team meeting he brought the matter slowly to a head as there was potentially much face to be lost and he did not wish to be on the wrong side of his boss when the awful truth came out in front of his subordinates.

As the situation slowly dawned on Turdivovich he kept glancing across at the computer and paper sorting system that had absorbed the station budget. As he brooded he became quieter and quieter. He was desperately trying to think what Michael Caine would do in this situation and he had a picture in his mind of a coach with a ton of gold overhanging the edge of a gorge in the Italian Alps. After much deliberation he rose deliberately to his feet and walked slowly to the telephone on the side table, savouring the moment.

"Listen Chaps," he said, picking up the handset, "I got an idea."

Then to the operator at the other end of the telephone - "Ask Wasim from the sewage treatment plant to join us."

A TIME AND A PLACE   BY JANE PETERS

It was just a normal patrol except that the lieutenant had left me with a small squad under the command of a corporal whilst he was liaising with another of the UN detachments. My cameraman had gone with him but I had come up here into the small village to see for myself how the villagers were handling the crisis. You have to be where the action is if you want to make the grade. If you're there when it's actually happening you get your own mention in dispatches.

So here I am, outside the shanty hall of some little village, just a mile out of town, where the remains of the large ethnic minority live; with just five squaddies and a corporal for company. We were lounging against the sandbag wall which protected the entrance to the building and I was enquiring why one of the soldiers had a different rifle? Foster, it transpired, was the regiment's champion shot and he preferred the older FN to the SA80 that has a reputation for misfiring – or not firing at all. But when the mob came over the brow of the hill towards us, we all went quiet and I realised that today, I had chosen the right place to be - right in the action.

There were probably about fifty of them and they had a variety of weapons from pitchforks to AK47's and other military hardware. They had broken off from the main group of militia who were much better armed and supported by vehicles. None of them was empty handed. As I looked at the approaching mob, with some considerable apprehension, a lowered voice spoke just behind me.

"Hi Kate, remember me?" it said in a distinct Midlands accent.

My name's not Kate but I knew he was addressing me - not only because I was the only female present - but because they refer to all the female correspondents as 'Kate' after Kate Adey. I turned and saw just another young squaddie in cammo's - with his face half blacked up - I certainly didn't recognise him and quietly told him so.

"I suppose your mate with the camera would remember me better - he got me and Gerry three months in Winson Green with that f****** video - remember now?"

Without looking I thought back to the time two years ago that I had been asked to cover an international match at Villa Park in Birmingham. It was at the time that Wembley Stadium was being rebuilt and the internationals were being held around the country. They had asked me to go because they had heard that there would be crowd trouble. The local fans had no reputation for violence but there were troublemakers coming to even up some old score with the foreign fans. Sure enough, in the Witton Road, we found a large group of hooligans taunting a group of the Dutch supporters who had strayed from the safe path to the stadium. The Netherlanders were trying to stay cool and just keep out of it but the troublemakers were having none of it.

Soon a stone was thrown and then a hail of bottles. I saw a young Dutchman being kicked on the floor whilst his mates backed away, not wanting to get involved. My cameraman recorded it all and a month later several of the miscreants were convicted of affray - mostly on the strength of our video evidence.

They say it's a small world and I was none too well pleased to find that my protectors, in this bedeviled country were renegades from prison. Without turning from the advancing crowd I asked him, "So how did you get here?"

"You heard the German Foreign Minister didn't you? [a recent press report] He reckons that half the British Army are recruited from jail. Both me and Gerry were given early release for joining up and we think Foster would have gone down if he hadn't - he's a Millwall supporter and they say they're all mad."

I looked back to the approaching crowd which grew ever more menacing. The corporal was preparing to make some sort of stand but I wished that the Lieutenant had been here with the Land Rover and the machine gun.

The corporal spoke quickly and quietly in a north-eastern accent to the five squaddies and I could only just make out what he was saying. He instructed them to remove their blue UN helmets and put their red regimental berets on. He told Gerry to drape his tee shirt over the sandbags behind them and as I saw the crude Union Jack I realised why. As I moved back behind the sandbags the corporal told them to act as if they were on parade and do exactly as he ordered - otherwise they might be going home in boxes.

"Stand tall, don't break ranks and don't run for cover. Stand in line two meters apart and aim just below the belt - make sure at least two of you are able to have a clear shot at the big guy in the centre. If he goes home the rest will follow."

"If I order 'open fire,' I shall break to your right so take out the ones with guns on the left of the crowd first". He finished the briefing with, "When I throw my bayonet down, I want to hear the safety catches off together - keep it tight."

"Foster," he called to the one with the FN, "get behind the wall and take aim on the front wheels of the Datsun over there. If I call your name take the front tyres out rapido! OK?"

The squaddie with the long gun nodded and took up his stance with the rifle held steady atop the sandbag wall. He sighted on the car about twenty meters away.

The corporal left us - me against the meager sandbag wall - the soldiers in line in front. The Muslim women in the school hall were starting to wail as they had now seen the mob that was now only thirty yards away. I said something to my squaddie about the corporal and how assured he looked.

"Coldstream Guard on attachment, Ma'am," he replied. "He's a Geordie who beat up his wife after she took a shine to someone else. They took away his stripes before attaching him to us to get him away from the base."

So in addition to my football hooligans the senior officer - a corporal - is a wife beater!

He strolled slowly up to the front of the oncoming crowd and held up his hand like a policeman commanding the traffic to stop. He had left his rifle behind but took with him the bayonet which he ostentatiously used to clean his fingernails.

"Any of you Dago's speak English?" he said with little respect for ethnic origins.

No one owned up so he continued as if they did. His strong Geordie accent seemed totally out of place and so unlike the groomed tones that the officers always used but he wasn't in the mood for niceties.

"Now look you f****** barbarians I want you all to piss off home - like now - and stop this f****** about …….. And if you don't I'm going to get really f****** angry." He stared at the big man in the centre who appeared to be the ringleader and held his stare for all of thirty seconds."

The big man spat on the ground and responded in a thick eastern European accent. "How are you going to do that?" he said, "your guns don't work and you don't know how to use them."

"Foster," shouted the corporal and two shots rang out about a second apart. The front wheels of the old Datsun exploded. As the local leader flinched the corporal threw the bayonet to stick point-down in the ground just two feet in front of him and I heard the clicks of the safety catches.

"If you pass that, Milo my son, you're dead."

The corporal calmly walked away exposing his back to them and the front of the mob to the five semi-automatic rifles.

I held my breath as the mob pondered their chances and then a murmuring began from behind. The ringleader half turned as if to answer and it was all over; they started to break up.

Within a few minutes they had disappeared from view on their way down to the town where the Dutch troops guarded the Muslim minority.

BANGERS AND MASH BY SHIRLEY KNOTT

Julian was 'in between' assignments with his usual program makers – an independent TV film maker of some repute – when he had a brainwave of how to fill in the gap.

Last week he had been motoring along the A446 to see an old friend in Lichfield and had passed an abandoned car parked in a lay-by. Today on his second visit he noticed that the bonnet of the car was up and it had lost several of its more transportable components. Funny that you never actually saw anyone taking anything off a car like this but it gradually withered away until the authorities saw fit to remove it to the breakers.

What if he made a documentary from secretly filming an abandoned car? - *The Demise of K549ANT* – he would think of a better title later. Make it so, he thought and started to set up his team as soon as he got home.

There were six of them so they could work shifts and they chose a lay-by on the A45 with a good hedge behind it. The farmer allowed access through his field and they set up a small portacabin with windows looking out towards the road. They carefully trimmed camera holes in the hedge and made an inconspicuous gap so that they could squeeze through to the lay-by.

They spent some time choosing the car and made someone's day by purchasing their 1983 Cavalier, which had seen better days but was still presentable. A week later they set up camp and Julian carefully positioned the car opposite the camera spy holes and Phil, the No1 cameraman, checked that they had a good view. When it was in position they settled down to watch.

That afternoon a police car stopped in the lay-by and ran a check to see if was stolen. After drawing blank the bobby placed a "Police aware" sticker on the rear windscreen and carried on, oblivious of the portacabin through the hedge. Having recorded this as filler material they snook out after 10 minutes and removed the sticker.

That morning, and each one thereafter, they celebrated the end of the nightshift by running back over the field to the adjacent transport café for breakfast. After a fad with bacon butties, bangers and mash became the favourite and they would wander back to the cabin with renewed energy.

That day and the next passed without any action and they were reduced to talking about their equipment and playing trivia games. Phil reckoned his camera cost over five grand and with the recorders and lighting equipment Julian had about £10k of equipment at his disposal – which explains why professionally produced videos don't look like home produced ones.

On day three a white pick-up stopped and the driver walked slowly round the Cavalier. He tried the locks and, on finding it locked, walked away and drove off. "Probably gone for reinforcements," said Phil, but at least they had something on film.

That afternoon another car stopped and two men, equipped with a metal coat hanger, approached the car. They soon had the passenger door open and then the bonnet. The battery was just out when Julian decided to do his Roger Cook impression and trotted out of the gap complete with microphone.

"Well what have we here?" he started but was totally flummoxed when the holder of the battery dumped it in his arms and made back to their car. They were gone in ten seconds flat.

"You made a right mess of that," said Phil, "jumped in too soon – and you have to cut them off from their car."

"So I'll do better next time." replied Julian.

His next attempt was a little better when two lads, also in a Cavalier, tried to remove the spare. They were surprised by Julian's intervention and tried to justify their actions.

"At last we're getting somewhere," thought Julian.

The next day was pure frustration as a number of cars stopped in the lay-by but none took anything from the Cavalier. As dawn approached on the fifth day Julian was exasperated and then it happened. A large low loader, with a powerful built-in crane, pulled off and maneuvered close to the car. The cameras whirred as they picked out the driver approach and inspect the Cavalier. He seemed to be reading something and after a few minutes he started to activate the crane. As he was attaching a cable to the car Julian jumped out to confront him. The light was now good and the cameras trained in on the confrontation with the sound coming over strong from the direction mike mounted on the roof of the cabin.

"Could you explain why you're stealing this car?" started Julian. He was completely flattened by the response.

"County Waste Disposal," retorted the low-loader driver "taking it to the pound."

"You can't do that," replied Julian, "it's my car and I want it here!"

"We're filming a documentary for television and the car is the subject."

"We'll see about that," said the driver as he pulled out a mobile phone. After a minute of muttering into the handset he informed Julian in no uncertain terms that the car had to go as it was considered a hazard and he had no choice in the matter.

Julian struggled back through the hedge with his tail between his legs.

"I've had enough," he said, "bangers and mash time."

They retreated to the café for breakfast after locking up.

They discussed what they had over breakfast and decided to call it a day. As there was no need for secrecy they abandoned their normal route over the fields and drove straight to the lay-by.

They were not surprised to find the low loader gone, as it had been over an hour since Julian had confronted the driver, but they were surprised to find the Cavalier still in position by the small gap in the hedge. Julian walked slowly round it expecting to find the wheels missing but it was just as they had left it.

With a growing sense of unease he slowly turned to peer through the gap in the hedge and confirmed his worst fears – the portacabin had gone.

THE KARMIC HOCKEY LEAGUE   BY ADRIAN SWALL

I returned home after three weeks working away and eagerly picked up the Hindu. After scanning the front page I turned to the sports pages at the back and found the Hockey results. Tigers had won 2-0 in Calcutta to gain revenge over the Chieftains who had beaten them 2-0 at home earlier in the season. After perusing the other results, I scanned the league and was relieved to find that the Chieftains would retain their third place with only one postponed game left to play in the whole season:

	P	*W*	*D*	*L*	*F*	*A*	*Points*
Bangalore Bankers	18	6	6	6	12	12	24
Bengal Tigers	18	6	6	6	12	12	24
Chennai Chieftains	17	6	6	5	12	10	24
Delhi Dashers	18	6	6	6	12	12	24
Hyderabad Harijans	18	6	6	6	12	12	24
Lucknow Lariats	18	6	6	6	12	12	24
Mumbai Marauders	18	6	6	6	12	12	24
Punjab Pundits	18	6	6	6	12	12	24
Uttar Pradeshis	17	5	6	6	10	12	21

I ploughed through the details of the other weekend results until I found what I was looking for at the very end…..

"The final match of the season will be played Saturday, 28th March at the Anna Salai Stadium where Chennai will host the much improved Pradeshis. The result is expected to be:

Chieftains – 0 Pradeshis – 2"

I didn't bother to go to the match.

BUSINESS AS USUAL BY JEAN-CLAUDE DUVALIER

Still inside the hangar, I climbed into the familiar cockpit; the plane now in high altitude decor with the 3rd Squadron identification letters still visible in outline along the side. "3-A-204" which makes my call sign 'Armada 204' but I don't expect there to be much conversation today - they don't speak much of my lingo and, despite the name 'Suarez' on my flying suit and helmet, I don't understand much Spanish. This means that if we do need to converse it will have to be (heaven help us) – in English!

I took off from Rio Grande military airfield early in the morning. Following the sinking of the Belgrano I don't think the Vincentio de Mayo is going to play any part in this conflict – at least they saved the planes by heading back into port. There are three A4s – Skyhawks – about 3,000 meters below me in visual range which form the basis of my protection and there will be others out of visual on my right flank. Getting more than ten aircraft up at the same time is a real struggle but today we managed it.

They call us 'technicians' just as the Americans used 'military advisers' in Vietnam and we're here to honor our contract for training and instruction – of course there's nothing like a live demonstration to improve the locals' level of competence. So here I am at 14,000 meters, all on my own, in my favorite plane. Having said that it has little combat capability and the Argie pilots hate it. How we ever managed to sell the Super Etendard to them I will never understand but then there's a lot more to these deals than meets the eye. They could have bought a lot more suitable combat aircraft – especially from the Ruskies – but no they had to get a highly specialised machine with virtually only one purpose – to launch the Exocet missile – but at that it excels.

Launching an AM39 'Exocet' (the best air-to-ship and ship-to-ship missile of its generation) is rather complicated even from a ground base but from an aircraft it takes years of training to get it right – hence the Argies' noticeable failure to get any hits on the British fleet.

Because it's designed to sink a ship, the missile is inevitably rather heavy and because it's designed for delivery by carrier-based aircraft it's only possible to carry one at a time. You can't sling it under the fuselage because of the clearance – so it has to go under the wing. You can hardly take off from a carrier with a two ton weight under one wing and nothing to balance it so we place a large drop tank of fuel under the other wing which enables us to fly further and more or less straight and true. However as we burn fuel the trim becomes more difficult and just when it's at its worst – at the limit of the aircraft's range – you have to fire the missile accurately to pick up the target selected off the Agave radar. This is not impossible but you also have to navigate yourself to the target besides contending with the BF radar warning system and the 3141 electronic counter measures pod - which is why most planes like this now carry a navigator/armourer. It's hardly surprising that the Argies prefer to bomb with 500 pounders from the Skyhawks!

Anyway the marketing department back home are less than pleased about the success rate of the launches and so they were looking for a 'more robust mission success ratio' which will inevitably increase sales to every country which is looking to take on its neighbour or even a second rate 'super-power'.

That's where we come in – the 'Three Musketeers' they call us: Jean-Luc, Jean-Louis and myself, Jean-Claude. We have flown Etendards from carriers all over the world; we are still, despite being past retirement age, regarded as some of the best strike pilots in the business. We have not, however, until we were 'invited to complete our training mission' that is, ever launched an Exocet against a live target under combat conditions.

I check on the multi-purpose Agave radar to see what's going on and run my checks on the Sagem attack system. As I can't yet see the forward picket there's not too much danger of anyone locking radar on to me yet but I switch on the BF radar warning system anyway. The A4s should take that pressure off me in any case.

I start to scan for the picket – the Royal Navy's forward scout which will pick up the attacking aircraft on its radar before they are apparent to the main task force. I suppose they drew the short straw just as I did today. But who will it be– one of the type 42 destroyers – Birmingham, Coventry, Glasgow? At least it won't be Sheffield – Jean-Luc put paid to her last week and since then they've put one of the more modern Broadsword class frigates to ride shotgun and give them better firepower. Sheffield's problem was that she could only hold her Sea Dart on to two attacking targets at a time – so when she was faced by three aircraft she had no chance. Even then we lost two of the three attacking Etendards - fortunately those flown by the local militants. Only Jean-Luc got back safely. Jean-Louis is not scheduled to fly his single 'contracted' mission until we know the result of mine. On reflection I suppose this is what the game is all about – it's no good developing all this new technology if you never have a chance to try it out under proper field conditions.

My mind wanders to the reports in the British press about the Belgrano. We need the Argies to get some success with the ship-borne version of the Exocet and she was the one to do it – or she would have been - but for Conqueror getting her oar in first. One of the Brits' own MPs is saying the she should not have been attacked as she was steaming away from the action. If only they could work out <u>why</u> she was heading back to the mainland - to come in helicopter range and pick up the only two guys who could enable them to fire their ship based Exocets! And who do you think they are? – Well they not called Carlos or Fernandez.

After what seems like an eternity I find the picket – probably a destroyer and a frigate but they are well off my beam. It's up to the A4's to deal with them and no doubt they already have Harriers from Invincible warming up their sidewinders to meet them. No heroics and dogfights – the taskforce aircraft don't want to mix it with the Argentine pilots in the Skyhawks who are renowned for the flying skill and bravery. The Harriers will take out as many as they can with their proximity fused sidewinders and go back to re-arm. The old F4's from Hermes will pursue the survivors and knock out as many as they can on the return run – assuming some have survived the wall of steel over the ships that they have bombed. The attrition rate is horrendous – worse than the Battle of Britain though the Argentine propaganda machine makes light of it.

I'm level with the pickets now, though they are masked from view by low cloud, and the radar profiles of the main task force are coming up in the long range view – of course if I can see them they can probably see me. I run over my launch check list again - everything must be just right. The missile must be dropped just inside its maximum range but I must get it away before the forward defences can take me down with their own missiles. Being on my own I am very vulnerable to any individual long-range missile if they launch it at the wrong time (for me that is). I descend to 10,000 meters to pick up a little speed and pray that they think I'm an A4 with a bomb – in that case they will keep their missiles in the launchers until later rather than risk missing me. I don't expect to be troubled by the sidewinders at this height but I am going to have trouble making out the targets.

My instructions are clear – I must attack one of the capital ships – not a destroyer or frigate – it must be Hermes or Invincible. There are three problems with this: firstly Hermes is tending to stay behind the shield of smaller ships and is difficult to get at; secondly making out which is Invincible, as its profile varies according to the counter measures and the helicopter decoys which throw out chaff; thirdly and this would be bad news – that I take out Canberra or Uganda – the Brits' hospital ships. Unfortunately my Exocet has to be launched well before I can have sight of the white ships with their red crosses and the task force does not transmit identification codes.

To counter this I have a precise briefing on today's set-up for the task force fleet. This must be based on the Brits' own data decoded at home or the US satellite data which (supposedly) only the Brits have access to. Either way there are four large profiles that I have to interpret. On my port and back a bit will be Hermes, to the centre will be Invincible and to the starboard will be Atlantic Conveyor. Canberra and the smaller Uganda will be in the centre well back behind Invincible. Of course the Conveyor being a large transport should show up much bigger and Invincible should show the smaller profile. Also the Conveyor has no defensive capability other than serving as an overnight 'car park' for the Harriers from Invincible. She should not, therefore, emit any offensive radar profile which is detectable on the BF.

I can now see the whole fleet on my long range radar and there, as expected, I can make out the pattern as outlined in this morning's briefing – I have been told to go after Hermes if she is still on the flank of the main fleet as this will give me the best chance of survival against the pursuing Phantoms that must already be taking off from her decks.

Port HERMES; Centre INVINCIBLE; Starboard CONVEYOR, rear CANBERRA – I go through the set-up again and confirm the match with the briefing. I am waiting for the final confirmation – a hostile radar lock from Hermes that will confirm that she is a combatant. I MUST NOT HIT CANBERRA!

The BF starts it warning tone and confirms the source as my intended target; I line up on the target and check that I am now well within range; every second of delay risks my own life and plane; I arm the Sagem attack computer and lock on to the left radar blip; the missile drops away and ignites. As the weight is lost from the right wing the plane bucks up and to the left; I pull hard on the stick and continue the left turn until the plane is heading back to the mainland; I jettison the drop tank from the left wing and accelerate to full power. The BF radar warning goes silent so they have probably locked on to the missile instead of me; I leave the ECM running whilst I make my way back past the picket which is still under attack from the A4s.

On landing I note more A4s taking off to attack the fleet. I want to wish them luck but my instructions are clear - talk to no one and do not leave the aircraft until told. After landing, I taxi into the back of the empty hanger and as the steps are rolled up the 'real' Suarez steps up to open the pod. I dismount and he takes my place. As I linger, out of sight, at the back of the hanger, he taxis the plane out through the front hanger doors where the Marshall of the Air Force and a group of politicians are waiting to greet him. There is a small crowd and they are cheering him; a politician is making a short speech to the TV cameras about the turning point of the war. This is the fourth time he has announced the sinking of HMS Hermes.

I change into my technicians' suit and walk back to the quarters. My colleagues have been watching the TV and monitoring the news. We can't get the BBC television or radio direct but we get the World Service patched through by the embassy. Everyone all over the world is talking about the Exocet missile.

I hear John Knott's words as he delivers the verdict on my mornings work.

"The Ministry of Defence wishes to announce, with great regret, the loss, this morning, at 0930 hours, of the Atlantic Conveyor …............"

Jean-Louis never got to fly his mission. The marketing department in Toulouse decided that the fallout from any bad publicity was too risky. Neither did we get congratulated for a job well done but that's the way things are. My motto is to just get on with things – anyway - I'm off to Baghdad for a holiday.

Business as usual?

WHAT'S IN A NAME? BY DON TWURRY

"How's it going?" I asked.

"We launched the pods last week," he responded, "without any publicity. After the furore during the debate we wanted to avoid any upsets. We hinted that it would be from Kennedy but actually they went from Vostok so that no one could interfere with things, you know what those Greenspeak people are like. We got the entangled particle message this morning to confirm that the deployment has taken place and your package has been safely delivered and deployed."

I was aware of the problems that had accompanied the programme and the bitter acrimony between the parties which had eventually been over-ridden at the highest level but only after a decade of dispute. Anyway nothing had prevented the probes from undertaking their journey to the adjacent star system and releasing their precious load of bacteria which would start the terra-forming process and make the planet available for future habitation.

Being responsible for the contents, but not the delivery, or even the justification, I was to some extent insulated from the anger which had erupted when the project had first been announced. I had carefully remained in the background, being acutely aware of the problems that could be created if my name came into the public arena. Death threats to me and my family were foreseen but forestalled simply by keeping the identities of everyone on the development team a strict secret.

Following a (quite) distinguished career in micro-biology and bacterial genetics, I had been given the job of designing the package which would deliver a cocktail of bugs to their 'new home'. Actually 'Newhome' was what we called it throughout the project and now that the trip was complete, I had been called upon to answer the all important question – what will be the name of this new planet which will make a home for our descendants, if many generations on?

He eventually put the question, hoping that I had already thought about it.

"Have you given any thought to the renaming Newhome now that the seeding process is underway?" he asked.

"Well I know that it's traditional to allow the spotters of new stars to name them but this is a little different," I responded, "I have given it some thought and even researched a little into the possibilities and decided on a nominal link to the source of my bugs as they have cost so much."

I didn't reveal, however, that the cultures, which cost over ten million dollars of the taxpayer's money, had been destroyed when one of the growing processes went catastrophically wrong and that I had replaced them with a spade full of soil dug up from my back garden.

"Come on," He said getting impatient, as he knew I had got something in mind and was anxious to know what would be the new name, "spit it out."

"Well last weekend I was tending the garden and I was thinking about the source of the cocktail of bugs which I put together and so I have named it in honour of the starring role which they will play."

"But what is it?" he countered impatiently.

"EARTH," I said.

COINCIDENCE   BY PYOTR

How is it that sometimes, not always of course, you find when away on holiday, that the people next to you on the beach live in the same street? It's actually not that unusual to meet a neighbour or a colleague when away from home but some things do seem so unusual that they appear to be more than a coincidence.

Was it a coincidence that William Shakespeare died on the same day of the year (23rd April) that he was born on? Or - that it's St George's day and he's buried in St George's church in Stratford. Actually dying on one's birthday happens to 1 in 365 of us every year. But it surely must be more than chance that Cervantes died on the very same day.

Is it a coincidence that my three grown-up children all live in fields? What - can't they afford houses I hear you say? Well it's simpler than that - the oldest one lives in Petersfield, the middle one in Northfield and the youngest in Macclesfield.

TRAVELLING BY NUMBERS

Back in the early days when we lived in Lancashire, we were taking my mother back home to the Midlands and decided to make a day of it going via North Wales. We stopped alongside a quiet country lane for a picnic but were disturbed by a stream of boy racers risking their lives along the narrow road. They were a sideshow from the Welsh Rally which was taking place about twenty miles to the South. When we rejoined the main road we were in heavy traffic, most of which was travelling in the same direction to watch a forest section of the rally. As we passed a lay- by my mother remarked that there were two identical cars parked and the drivers were talking to each other alongside one of the cars. They were both bright yellow Austin Sprites, one with a hardtop and the other a soft top which was up. As we travelled south they caught up and the leading one overtook us; the other one followed behind. After a few minutes, I asked my wife to read out the number plate on the car behind. "CWW160", she replied. I asked her to confirm and then view the number plate on the car in front. "CWW160", she replied. Now I never found out what the drivers of the two Sprites were up to but it certainly was not a coincidence.

A NEAR MISS

Later in life I met someone in Blackpool who has remained a good friend to this day. We swapped stories about the past and he told me how he had built the bridges along the M4. We had both studied civil engineering and, before being persuaded to go to Manchester, I had been awarded a place at Aston where he went. Had I taken up my place there we would have been in the same year on the same course. A minor coincidence or just chance?

GLOVES, FOOD MIXERS AND TWEEZERS

And there are little things that occur and are often forgotten about because they lack significance.

I was visiting a friend near Reading and had some time to spare so I decided to photograph the centre of Henley on Thames. It was market day and very cold so I put my leather gloves in my side pocket and put on the thin cotton gloves that I wore when using the camera. I left the car park and wandered around the town taking pictures of the older buildings. When I decided that I had had enough, I took off my thin gloves and rooted in my pocket to find the thicker leather ones. I was a little dismayed to find that I had only one and had obviously lost the other. After a warming cup of soup, I made my way back to the car park and as I approached the car I saw a black leather glove on the ground close the rear door of my car. I stooped to pick it up thinking this must be where I had dropped it but when I tried to put it on I found it was much too small. It was not my glove.

Years ago, I used to enter the competitions that were run by retailers to promote their goods. So I was a little disappointed when I won a food mixer about a month after we had bought one. Not long afterwards there was a country-wide promotional competition run by Pedigree Petfoods which involved collecting the labels from their tins and posting them in by a certain date. The published list of prizes was very impressive including cars as top rewards. As, at that time, we were working with an animal charity, I 'bought' all of their labels and had an enormous pile to send. We waited with baited breath for the publication of the list of prize winners and got more and more despondent looking down the list until we spotted our name – we had won a food mixer.

A few years later we were parking the car in Oxford city centre close the theatre where Denis Loccorier was to give a concert. I went to the pay-and-display machine and bought a ticket which I took back to put in the windscreen. As I placed it there was a gust of wind which enabled the ticket to slide down one of those narrow gaps which you get around the dashboard of a car. I could see the edge of the ticket but could not reach it. My wife looked at it and proffered the advice that I needed a pair of tweezers. I thought for a short while and then remembered that I had a first aid kit in the boot which might include one. I walked round the back of the car and was amazed to see a pair of bright steel tweezers lying there on the ground.

THE BIG MATCH

One of my jobs, in the water industry, concerned new technology and I got a trip to Guernsey to look at the digital mapping system which they had introduced. I was accompanied by a computer specialist from ICL who was responsible for the software. Over dinner that evening we had a bottle of wine and talked about business and our backgrounds. We soon discovered that we had been at Manchester University at the same time – me doing civil engineering and him reading maths. We then talked about the halls we had stayed in – me at Montgomery House and him at Dalton Hall. We discovered that we had both played soccer for our respective halls and I asked about the big grudge match in 1963 between the two halls on which the destination of the 'Torrington Trophy' depended. He remembered it well and the furore it had created as Dalton had a professional playing for them. We were struggling to keep up and were losing 1-0 at half time but Jim, our skipper, said that the opposition were in danger of falling apart as he heard one of the full backs remonstrate with their professional captain who had been issuing orders as if he were a sergeant major. "If you shout at me like that again I'll kick you in the balls," is what was reportedly said. I related the tale and he laughed. "That was me." he said. The match ended 1-1.

LONDON PRIDE

After my first 'retirement' I worked for the international branch of the company. I was tasked with taking some bid documents to South Africa for signing by our partner company. My boss, Henry, an expert in manipulating the system had booked me onto a flight with Virgin Atlantic just after they had introduced their *Premium Economy* class. You got most of the advantages of business class without the exorbitant cost. The flight was fairly empty for some reason and I was given seat J8 which was a window seat at the front of the new class and I was the only one in the row. After takeoff, the stewardess came through the curtains from the galley and asked what I would like to drink. "Have you any beer?" I asked. "Yes, London Pride," she replied "– would you like two?" "Thank you." I said and enjoyed a very pleasant flight. After delivering the documents and getting them signed I had a day off before flying back. On the return flight I sat in seat J8 and again had the row to myself. After takeoff, the stewardess came through the curtains from the galley and asked what I would like to drink. "Have you any beer?" I asked. "Yes, London Pride," she replied "– would you like two?" "Thank you," I said and then asked her if she had seen me before. "Oh," she said – "you were in the same seat two days ago and we had the same conversation." Déjà vu perhaps but hardly a coincidence.

TRAFFIC

I didn't enjoy my final year at university; I found the course content irrelevant for a practising engineer and did as little as I could to get by. The exception was traffic engineering which had just been added to curriculum but was not considered to be a real 'engineering' subject. We had to choose a subject for our third year dissertation and, after some trouble, I managed to wangle a project concerning the speed/flow relationship of moving traffic. After some observations on Princess Parkway, and a lot of research into papers on the subject, I determined that the prevailing opinions about it were wrong. The TRRL (now TRL) had the graphical relationship as a straight line but this was only half of the story. I proposed that the straight line was, in fact, just part of a curve which had to go back on itself to join the origin. Proving this would take a lot of time but my conclusion was accepted and my dissertation was amongst the best presented.

Some years later, I was working in Trinidad and was discussing engineering with some other professionals over a few beers. One of them told me he was a traffic engineer and I mentioned my college project. "Yes," he said, "that's how it is in the text books now – it's actually a parabola."

My next project was in Guyana and the staff had asked me to umpire their annual cricket match between the two main offices. I agreed but thought I should brush up on the laws and asked if there was a book shop where I might get something to help. I entered the only technical bookshop in Georgetown through the front door and was confronted by rows of book shelves. Something caught my eye on the top row of the first shelf and I stopped to pull it out – *Highway Traffic Analysis and Design, Third Edition' by Soulter and Hounsell*. It opened at page 129 and I was confronted, at the top of the page, with a diagram of my parabola.

THE HUNTSMAN

When we did our world tour and spent time with relatives in Melbourne, we were taken out for a meal at a very nice restaurant on the final evening of our stay. For some reason, halfway through the main course, I turned and noticed a very large spider approaching my seat along the floor. The room was air conditioned and quite cold so the spider was moving quite slowly. Excusing myself, I took the large ashtray from the centre of the table and gently placed it over the animal to prevent it getting lost amongst the diners. As the waiter came past I told him there was a large spider beneath the ashtray and he gently removed it outside where he let it go. He explained that it was a Huntsman and, whilst they were poisonous, they rarely bothered humans, preferring to scuttle away.

On our return, I offered to take my sister out for lunch on her birthday and she decided to take us to an unusual pub on the outskirts of Worcester. We travelled a few miles into the country and went across a narrow bridge over the M5. When we came to the pub I found it was called 'The Huntsman' and I was reminded of the enormous spider in Australia. We had lunch.

Two years later (not actually to the day) I was invited to go to a beer and skittles do and, never having done it before, I agreed. Then I discovered that I had been invited because I would be driving as my friend did not have his car on the road. He didn't know what the pub was called or where it was precisely but he had instructions on how to get there. We drove down the M5 to Worcester and then took the A38 to Kempsey. At the Post Office, he told me to turn left and we wandered along a dark country lane for a couple of miles. As we crossed the M5 on an overbridge, I got a feeling of déjà vu. As we pulled up in the car park I read the sign – 'The Huntsman'.

CNICT

Many years ago, when my hobby was photography, I went with a photographic club to North Wales for a long weekend. The main attraction was a day-long visit to the slate quarry above Trawsfynneth and the weather was good. This is a haunting place which is a favourite with Midlands' photo clubs as it offers so many wonderful scenarios. We got lots of good pictures amongst the ruined buildings and slate tips and then wandered to the far side of the site. We came to an almost sheer edge and looking over there was the remains of the incline where the bogies took the slate down the valley to a narrow gauge railway which would take it the docks for export. I wanted to explore but the rest of the group thought that the weather was deteriorating and wanted to get back to the town. I stood at the edge of the incline looking down on the valley below and vowed to come back.

Many years later, in Wales, I went out to walk in the snow which covered all of the mountain tops but not the valleys. We went to a small car park and I was told how, because of its shape, Cnict was known as the Welsh Matterhorn. We set off and as we started up the 'mountain' (it's actually less that 1,000 ft high) we found ourselves in the snow. It was a crisp clear day and we could see that only one pair of walkers had gone before us. We followed their tracks straight up the near side and reached the top in less than an hour. After a short break we carried on along the ridge which lies at the back of the mountain and walked for quite some time until I started to experience a feeling of déjà vu. It became clear to me, as we approached some derelict buildings, that I had seen them before – even photographed them? As we got amongst them, I looked back at the way we had come up from the valley and saw that I was at the top of the incline where the slate was taken out for export.

LIZZIE'S COTTAGE

We booked a cottage near Beddgellert and enjoyed a long weekend of walking in the hills and up a nearby mountain. I found the cottage unusual to say the least and thought I might return there one day – as you do when you've had a nice experience somewhere. I slept in a bed which was situated on a sort of mezzanine floor with an open front onto the main living area. I found it strange but slept well so put it down as an experience. A year later, I visited my friend Lizzie and after dining we talked over a bottle of wine and caught up on what we had been doing and where we had been. As usually happens, this kind of conversation tends to concentrate on holidays and such. So it was no surprise that Lizzie told me how she and a group of friends had hired a holiday cottage in North Wales. Eager to swap notes as I had been to Snowdonia the previous year, at my prompting, she described the cottage and then, to her surprise, I described the route to it and then the strange layout with the half upstairs bedroom. It transpired that we had slept in the same bed, a year apart.

MASTER OF THE UNIVERSE

I went to work in Mexico City and did not know anyone in the team over there, however, I soon found most of my colleagues were sociable and we often went out to eat in the evenings. One night, a colleague and I went to an Argentine restaurant in the Polanco district and swapped notes on our careers. He was about 15 years younger than me but we had both qualified as civil engineers and gone on to specialise in water. After a while I asked him what had made him decide to become an engineer. Almost without hesitation he said that it was the way he was taught to love maths and this was down to him having been taught by the best maths master in the world.

"No," I responded, "you can't have had the best maths teacher because I did."

"Where did you go to school?" he asked.

"Hartlebury," I replied, "and where did you?"

"Halesowen," he said …….and you can see what's coming……we both had the same maths teacher but some years apart – ' a true master of the universe'!

4, DUNLEY ROAD

I was brought up on a council estate in Stourport on Severn and my mum worked as a cleaner/housekeeper for a family who lived about a mile away on a road with very nice 'bought' houses. Their house, No.4, Dunley Road was quite big and obviously built for a well-off family as it had a servants' bell system in the kitchen. It was owned by the Campbells; he was chief colourist at the local carpet factory and she was a teacher.

Years later, when I worked in project appraisal I had to meet up with an engineering consultant at the company offices in Burton on Trent. After we had concluded the business we went for lunch in a cafeteria overlooking the river and got talking about our respective careers; both being civil engineers. After university I had gone into local government and then the water industry whereas he had always worked for consultants.

I then lived in Coventry and he informed that, having taken up a new post in Birmingham, he had bought a house within commuting distance to the west. It transpired that he had moved to Stourport and when I asked where, he told me that he had bought a very nice house – the first one he looked at – from a Scottish couple who had recently retired.

"Was their name Campbell?" I asked.

"Yes." he replied, "How did you know?"

He had bought No.4, Dunley Road.

LUCY BALDWIN IN EGYPT

My employers asked me to go to Egypt to prepare a proposal for a training scheme to be set up at a new centre in the Nile Delta. I had some difficulties engaging with the local support as all of them appeared to need to be elsewhere when they were most wanted. After a week of frustration, we were invited to join a tour of the water facilities which served the area, which would give us a clearer picture of the training needs. I was, therefore pleased to meet a fellow Brit on the coach and introduced myself as we walked around the water treatment plant.

"Hello, I'm Pyotr and I'm representing Severn Trent International."

"Hi, Pyotr, I'm Frank and I'm with Thames Water."

After discussing the various stages of treatment and the state of the plant, we were offered refreshment and sat down in the shade. I noticed that Frank was a similar age as me and after swapping notes on our careers, I asked him where he came from.

"Oh, a little place in the Midlands that you won't have heard of," he said.

"Try me," I responded, "I'm from the Midlands myself."

"A small town in Worcestershire called Stourport." he replied.

"I know it well," I said. "I was born there – so when were you born?"

"May 1943," he responded, "In the Lucy Baldwin Maternity Home."

"Great," I replied, "I was born there in April 1943."

In all my time abroad I have never met, before or since, anyone from the same place and so near as regards their date of birth.

SOMERSET LEVELS

The Levels suffered severe flooding in the winter of 2014/15 and being a (retired) water engineer I set about looking at the problem in detail. All of the public and press were moaning about the lack of dredging on the River Parrett and would not accept the view that, as a tidal river, it would have made no difference. I bought a detailed OS map and set about plotting the extent of the inundation and looking at the infrastructure. I soon noticed that the solution did not involve the rivers at all but the main overflow channel the 'King's Sedgemoor Drain' which discharged excess flows to the lower reach of the tidal Parrett. The problem was that the 'Drain' only discharged at low tide so was unable to cope with the vast volume of flood water. I determined that the solution was to install pumps on the outfall of the drain and this was eventually done.

During the spring, I went with my walking companion, to see the Levels for myself and visit the key points. We parked near Burrow Mump which had featured heavily in the television coverage of the flooding and followed a circular route along the Parrett and then the River Tone, returning along a narrow country road which ran parallel to the river. At one point we stopped and admired a small garden which was quite immaculate, unlike the others along the road. I noticed that the raised bank at the back of the garden was actually the bank of the River Tone and I discussed whether it would be reasonable to knock on the door and ask to have a look at the river. We decided it would not and continued on our walk.

Several years ago, I joined 'Friends Reunited' and contacted a few persons who I had known in my school days. One was my girlfriend from junior school who I had not seen since we split up after 'eleven plus'; she went to the girls' High School and I went to the boys' Grammar School. After a few years exchanging pleasantries, I asked if she would like to meet up and asked where she lived. "I live in the Somerset Levels," she replied, "but you don't need to worry about the floods as it's all gone now." She gave me her address and we arranged to meet in the car park of the pub in Burrowbridge. We exchanged car registrations so that we could recognise each other, not having met for nearly 60 years.

I drove down from the Midlands and, being an hour early, I decided to find her house. The complication was that I had left the paper with her address on it at home but I could remember the car number. I drove about four miles along a narrow road which I eventually realised was the one which we had walked along last year. I spotted her silver hatchback parked alongside the road and as I maneuvered into the vacant space behind, the door of the adjacent cottage opened and a lady looked out. "Pyotr?" she asked and I nodded. She came across the perfect little garden to greet me – it was the one we had stopped by last year.

THE HOUSE IN BALSALL COMMON

In the early 1970s we lived in Coventry and, having failed to get the school place that we wanted for our eldest son, we set about moving house to a catchment with expectations more in line with our own. After a few failures, we were shown round a bungalow in Balsall Common by a charming lady and we decided that we liked it. The sun was shining and she was so engaging and cheerful that we decided that we would buy it. Looking at the façade we were taken with the idea that it looked a little like a Spanish hacienda and we could achieve that look by replacing the grey slate tiles with orange pantiles. The day after we made an offer, subject to survey, and this was accepted.

I briefed our solicitor and engaged a local surveyor to carry out a full survey of the bungalow as it had been altered by the man of the house who was a builder. They wanted to move quickly as the lady of the house was pregnant and did not want to be moving around the time she would give birth.

We arranged for a second visit and went back. The lady had already moved to her mother's as she did not wish to give birth at the house. It was a dull day and the husband showed us round. When we entered the dining room, which was a single story extension, with an old oak door, I got the strangest feeling - that there was someone behind me. He explained that the floorboards and door had been rescued from an old property which had been demolished in nearby Temple Balsall. Outside there was an oval swimming pool but it was empty and neglected – due to a crack in the concrete we were told. Under the dining room was a garage which we could hardly make out as the light did not work. Again, I had a sense of foreboding.

That night my wife had a severe nightmare and when questioned, she related it to the house which we were considering buying. She had a strong sense that something bad would happen to us if we bought it and asked me to reconsider. I responded that we should at least hear what the surveyor had to say and then we would decide whether to proceed.

The surveyor rang and asked me to go into his office later that day. As soon as I sat down he indicated sheets of notes which were the list of numerous faults. He started by asking if we were determined to buy the property as it had so much wrong with it. In addition to the 'Gerry built' extension, the lounge window was unstable and much remedial work was required. He then went quiet, almost conspiratorial, and suggested that there might be something underlying the lack of care. I asked him what he meant and he responded that he had had the most unusual feeling when he entered the dining room. The hairs had stood up on the back of his neck and he had suffered a cold shudder down his spine. I asked what he thought had caused this and, after a long deliberation, responded – the floorboards. There's something evil attached to them. We decided not to proceed.

The year afterwards, I was in the area and drove past the house. I was gratified to see that the new owners had seen the same potential as we had and had converted the roof covering to Spanish pantiles. It had a distinct 'hacienda' look.

As our children grew up we settled into our new house in Solihull and entered the 'taxi driver' stage of life where you seem to spend all of your spare time ferrying children around. Saturday morning was the time for swimming lessons and I was sat up in the viewing area overlooking the pool when I spotted a colleague from work who was there with his own children. I struck up a conversation and we chatted for while; I explained that we had moved to Solihull for the schools and he informed me that he had moved to Balsall Common for the same reason. He lived in School Road – near where the bungalow that we nearly bought stood. I mentioned the improvements and how nice it looked.

"Yes," he replied, it was bought by a very nice couple who spent a lot of money doing it up but, tragically, they both died shortly afterwards."

WHAT OF IT?

Well, nothing much; we have all experienced coincidences in the course of our lives and they do give us food for thought and even something a little different to talk about in the long winter evenings. Hope you enjoyed mine.

NOTES ON RECENT HISTORY   BY JANE PETERS

Wow! What a privilege. I have been invited along by the Ministry of Culture to write up the recent history of the conflict. They envisage a book plus a full length film in colour. The only problem I have is that my German is not as good as it should be despite having a day a week one-to-one tutelage over the last month. I really should go to live there for some time in order to pick up the day-to-day nuances which can be so confusing in such a technical language.

Conversely, being a lecturer in European history in Oxford, I am ideally placed now that it has become the capital of the country and all of the Ministries are located here in the college buildings which housed the students until six months ago. Obviously London remains the biggest center of population and the financial hub but the power of government is now here.

My interview was with Rommel when he came over to satisfy himself that everything was set up properly – all shipshape and Berlin fashion. He was most charming though not in the best of health. I think he has limited time left so wants his version of events accurately recorded. After talking about my background and experience he confirmed my appointment which was a considerable relief after the colleges here were all disbanded. Of course Cambridge is different as Werner Heisenberg has taken over there and converted the entire campus into a scientific research center. The upheavals have put all of us in a nervous frame of mind though it is now clear our new masters are keen to make the most of our academic institutions.

And now I have the chance to write up history with one disturbing thought in the back of my mind. They say that history is written by the winners and the losers get no say. How I deal with this is my own problem but my first talk with Herr Rommel bodes well. He has warned me not to take all that I am told at face value especially from Goebbels and Himmler. He and Doenitz should be accurate and truthful but I am to take Goering with a pinch of salt. There will be no input from the Fuhrer due to the poor state of his health. In fact he may not even be alive. All of those concerned are to make themselves available whenever I need them and to set a good example Herr Rommel will set aside two hours each day for the next two weeks to start off the process. I should look to submit early drafts of my manuscripts for review by Goebbels in just two months.

What follows is a series of extracts from my notes based on the conversations with Herr Rommel. They are not in chronological order so the timescales might be somewhat confusing and there are many things which need to be cross checked with others when I get to interview them. Please accept my apologies for that. I started out taking notes but then Herr Goebbels gave me a recording machine which I now use. I had a choice between a Telefunken and a Grundig; choosing the latter as it is more compact. Hence some of the paragraphs are as recorded verbatim on tape and others are as taken down by hand.

[The notes which follow in parenthesis are reminders to me about cross checking with other relevant figures and are not part of the narrative]

Following the resignation of Chamberlain there was a clear conflict between the doves (represented by Halifax) and the hawks (who favoured Churchill). Halifax was put forward by Chamberlain as his successor and accepted the post despite being a member of the Lords. Most saw Churchill as the natural leader and one to unite the country but others saw him as a bull in a china shop who might bring the country to its knees. Halifax promptly appointed Churchill as War Minister in order to quell dissent. So Winston had control of the armed forces and day-to-day conduct of the war but not the politics. The German High Command rejoiced on hearing the news as they had feared that Churchill would be their main antagonist. Hence Germany considered this decision as being very much in their favour; it would not alter the defeat of Britain but it might mean fewer casualties in bringing it about. Hess was sent over to commence negotiations and Halifax received him in London. The talks, however, failed and Hess returned without any clear idea of the British Government's stance; much to the Fuhrer's dismay. [Confirm with Hess]

The King is in his castle. Actually he is not. Buckingham Palace is now a military hospital and Windsor Castle has been appropriated by the Gestapo as their British headquarters; hence the King has been installed in Blenheim

Palace which, conveniently, is just up the road from here. He will be crowned, Edward VIII, next year in Christ Church Cathedral along with Queen Wallis. Having been rescued, from imprisonment by the British Government in The Bahamas, last year the King had been living at his old address near Paris before being flown in to Britain following the cessation of hostilities. His rescue by the SS and subsequent journey by U Boat is a story in its own right. [Doenitz has already written this up]

The continuation of the House of Windsor is not in doubt as the two princesses are already next of kin to Edward. They will return from school in Bavaria for the coronation and we have a member of the Greek aristocracy in mind as suitor for one of them. The whereabouts or fate of their parents remains unclear though there are strong rumours that they are in Australia. Earlier indications suggested Canada but this was denied following the US invasion of the Dominium which was welcomed with open arms there. The family name will revert to Saxe-Coburg following the coronation and it is expected that the Greek Prince, who is suitor to one of the princesses, will be promoted in the order of accession following his marriage. [Confirm with Royal correspondent]

Most people think that work started on the atomic bomb after the war had started but, actually, Heisenberg and company were well up to speed by the start of the war. He had two big problems. Firstly was the lack of resources and secondly the loss of scientists who had left to work in the US. Both of these situations were the fault of the Fuhrer as he had not seen the value of the atomic bomb; he simply did not believe that it would work and hence did not provide adequate funding. His persecution of the Jews meant that many prominent Jewish academics went abroad especially those following Einstein to the USA. We were only able to solve the issue when the Fuhrer became too ill to govern and we were able to reverse the doctrine of 'The Final Solution'. [Himmler and Heisenberg]

The Swiss and Spanish Ambassadors in Washington were briefed by von Ribbentrop and dispatched to see the Secretary of State and then President Roosevelt himself. They were to explain the situation with the Fuhrer's illness and our proposals to alleviate the matter concerning the Jews. A delegation of American Jews was to come to Europe and witness the truth about the fate of their fellows which (we said) had been seriously misrepresented in the States. This was agreed to and they duly arrived in Germany via Switzerland. We showed them the concentration camps, the gas chambers and all the horrors we could think of and then offered them a deal. All this would stop if they would act to keep America out of the war and in return, we would give a solemn undertaking not to invade Britain. After a day of debate and some delay, they agreed on one further condition – that we would mirror the British undertaking of 1919 and set up an independent state of Israel in the area currently known as Palestine. We agreed subject to a further condition of our own – that a prominent young scientist called Robert Oppenheimer would return to Gottingen University and take the Chair of Physics there. [See ambassadors]

The US was appraised of these matters and readily agreed as this would leave them free to concentrate their attention of the growing threat from Japan. Obviously we were aware of the possibility of a pre-emptive strike on Pearl Harbor but did not communicate this to the Americans. Oppenheimer reluctantly returned to his alma mater and he was placed under the care of Werner Heisenberg. Niels Bohr was intercepted in a small boat attempting to cross the Baltic to Sweden. He was offered a place at Gottingen in return for cessation of the anti Jewish programme in Denmark. So the Gottingen Group was reassembled with a powerful team of scientists who were able to proceed with utmost alacrity on the development of the atomic bomb. [Talk with Heisenberg and Oppenheimer]

Britain had set up a code breaking operation in a village in Buckinghamshire which was entrusted with the task of breaking our ENIGMA codes. This entailed building replicas of our encoding machines and, after breaking the secret of how the codes worked, building more machines which could be used by them to decode our messages. Our spies alerted us to the progress being made and we were dismayed to find that they were already well on the way to working out how the machines worked but had not thus far succeeded in deciphering any of our messages. We ascertained that the main threat came from a young mathematician who had acquired one of our coding machines via Poland. Our contacts informed us that he was a homosexual so we set him up for an encounter and then informed the authorities who had him arrested and bailed. Whilst on bail we entrapped him again and they then imprisoned him. He was released shortly after agreeing to treatment but the episode ruined his career and the code breaking went downhill from there on. [Bletchley Park files?]

Our coding systems were always superior to the British ones which we had little trouble breaking. However, at the start of the war each branch of our services had their own department responsible for deciphering British and other Allied messages. As soon as I took over, I amalgamated them into a single organisation modeled on Bletchley Park. [BP again]

After our successes in Europe under the Fuhrer, we were coming to a halt and my own campaign in North Africa went horribly wrong. After I won several battles we suffered a relatively minor defeat and this resulted in the Fuhrer indulging in an enormous sulk. He basically refused us resources and the interference with our supply lines from Allied forces in Malta meant that we suffered badly. This sent the British morale soaring and ours plummeted as we had not been defeated on land up until then. I returned to Berlin and went to confront Hitler but found him strangely distracted. I sought help and his doctors diagnosed Parkinson's disease. We sent him to hospital and I set about reorganising things. I contacted Doenitz and Speer who both agreed to back me up and then confronted Goering. Without the Army (which I controlled), the Kriegsmarine (which Doenitz had control of) and aircraft (which Speer controlled the production of), he would be unable to continue the war with just the Luftwaffe. So he reluctantly joined with us. [Check with Goering, Speer and Doenitz]

We got von Ribbentrop, Himmler and Goebbels together and told them we had organised a coup; We (myself, Doenitz and Goering) would rule as a military junta with them in control of ministries. They could join us or die. They joined us and we organised the assassination of Heydrich in Czechoslovakia. The Fuhrer was left as titular head of state and Hess continued as Deputy Fuhrer in order to keep him in the loop. The first thing we did was to halt the Jewish pogroms and forced deportation to the camps. All extermination was put on hold pending a visit by a delegation from the US who came to see the camps for themselves. We hid nothing and showed them the true horrors which had been undertaken so far. They were not aware of the problem with the Fuhrer's health and so thought that the extermination would continue unless something was done to stop it. We did nothing to disabuse them and blatantly used the fate of their fellows to pressurise them. We succeeded and they were able to keep the US from declaring war on us and we undertook (quite seriously) not to invade Britain. They were not aware that we hoped to achieve the collapse of Britain without an invasion as we would by then have our new weapons which could raise whole cities. [Himmler and Goebbels]

Once the bomb had been developed, we soon realised that our proposed V1 rockets would not be able to carry it. It was far far too heavy and, even after we developed the V2, we would not have a delivery system. So we took a leaf from the Brit's book and resorted to subterfuge. Our aim was to get at least two of the new bombs into British cities and only let them off if we had too. The task was delegated to

Doenitz as the only one with the capability to carry such loads. [See Doenitz]

The rocket programme, under Wernher von Braun, was eating up a disproportionate share of resources. Much of the manual work was being done, initially at least, by slave labour which was resulting in thousands of deaths. This ceased when we stopped the exterminations and it was decided that the programme would continue but only in the background as our statisticians informed us that the effort of building the rockets was greater than the damage they would inflict.

We had another big problem – where to test the bomb? Heisenberg was reluctant to carry out any sort of test as that would mean that the effort of building the test bomb (which was enormous) would be wasted. He was sure that it would work so he insisted that we deploy the first bomb and use it on the enemy. Our biggest problem was still the Fuhrer's disastrous decision to invade Russia. We were tied down near Stalingrad and at Leningrad whilst the fierce Russian winter was taking a greater toll on our forces than the Russians themselves. This possible test provided an opportunity on the Russian plain where we had planned to eliminate the Russian tanks in a massive battle. Personally, I thought that our technical superiority would be overcome by the Russians superiority in numbers. According to our intelligence, they had over six thousand T34 tanks to our four thousand Panzers. Our supply lines were stretched but theirs were not and they had fuel to burn whilst we were always short of petrol and diesel.

Our plan was to lure the Russian forces into a clear area, ideal for a tank battle, near Kirsk and then confront them. The commanders were informed to go ahead with their planning but to adapt the tactics to include a rapid withdrawal. We also substituted many of our battle tanks with over a thousand decoys which looked similar but were only capable of movement and firing blanks from a mock gun. This is something we learned from the British who often employed subterfuge on the battlefield and elsewhere. So, having delayed the battle by a couple of weeks, we then built a substantial tower and Heisenberg's test bomb was put on top. A mock radar scanner was placed in front and we let it be known through their spies that we intended to control the battle through a radar based command system which would give us a tactical advantage.

When the battle did commence we feinted and made some little gains where the superiority of our tanks was apparent but then fell back. Our second line was defended by the mock tanks many of which were driven by volunteers from the Hitler Youth. The Russian tanks made easy meat of them and were drawn on towards our 'radar' tower. They desperately wanted to capture this intact as they had no radar capability themselves and this would give them a massive leap forward. They easily passed the tower as, by then, our main forces had fallen back over twenty kilometers and were not even in sight let alone range. When the bomb was triggered the explosion was so massive that even some of our observation posts were destroyed. The opposing forces were totally annihilated and, soon after, we were offered terms on an organised withdrawal from Russian territory. This was agreed though we kept Ukraine. [Need field commanders' names]

We were always aware of Churchill's double and kept careful track of his movements as well as those of the man himself. His trips to America were observed but we had already taken the sting out of his tail with our secret agreement concerning the Jews. Where is he now – still alive - you ask? Yes, indeed, though you will have to take my word for it that it is him and not the actor who masqueraded as him so well. He lives in retirement in Kent at a place called Chartwell which he bought back in the 1920s. This was his reward for signing the cease fire. [Visit Chartwell]

This brings me to your own demise. As you recall, we had delegated the responsibility for delivery of the devices to the Kreigsmarine and they came up with the scheme to attack Portsmouth. A task force was assembled consisting mainly of redundant warships and volunteer crews. We would drive straight up Spithead and demolish the home port of the British Navy. Gneisenau had been badly damaged in a storm but was seaworthy and accompanied by Prinz Eugen with six destroyers they made a formidable force. A dozen E Boats had been adapted to overshoot the submarine boom and would draw fire from the shore batteries. The Luftwaffe got every serviceable aircraft flying to attack Manston and Biggin Hill as a diversion for the RAF who were subsequently unable to defend Portsmouth. The destroyers had specialist equipment to disable the submarine boom which enabled Gneisenau and Prinz Eugen to enter Spithead. [Actually, he confided as an aside that it was a lucky salvo from the Prinz which sank the Hood, not Bismarck. [check with Doenitz] They did not last long as the British Navy soon awoke to the threat and had ships rapidly responding. But Gneisenau and her escort were only a decoy. Once the boom had been disabled a U Boat entered and made for the entrance to Portsmouth Harbour. She partially surfaced, as planned, opposite Gosport and immediately detonated the bomb. The resulting tidal wave wiped out all of the warships on both sides and the whole of Portsea Island. [Consult Dowding and Mountbatten]

Following the destruction of Portsmouth we used the American Ambassador to approach Halifax. He was informed that a recently arrived Panamanian freighter, currently moored in the East India Docks contained a similar device which was booby trapped to go off if interfered with. It would devastate the whole of the East End and possibly much more. Also a submarine, similar to the one which had just devastated Portsmouth, was submerged just a kilometer off Leith. With the threats to London and Edinburgh, Halifax capitulated and resigned handing power over to Churchill who, on the advice of Roosevelt, signed the surrender document the next day. As you see, we didn't need to invade; the outcome of the war was ordained as soon as Heisenberg had perfected his design of the bomb. [Confirm with American Ambassador]

Our work setting up the Nationengemeinschaft is proceeding well under the auspices of Herr Himmler and von Ribbentrop. Firstly we cancelled all institutions concerned with the old British Empire and gave all of their territories the option of becoming independent or joining our new Commonwealth. This may sound a little over generous but, quite honestly, we do not have the manpower to absorb them all. Conditional upon joining is the introduction of German as the second language and the phasing out of English in all schools. This was no problem in East Africa and Namibia as they had, prior to WWI, been closely allied with the Fatherland and some were even part of our own Empire. South Africa warranted a special arrangement whereby they were granted membership through an associate setup with the Dutch Government which had become an autonomous region of the Reich. Similar arrangements were made with the French and Belgian colonies. India has become independent. Australia and New Zealand declined any contact with us and are negotiating a treaty with the US and the newly absorbed Canada. The situation in France is unresolved as, unlike Britain, most of it was taken by force and de Gaulle is proving problematical about the return of their gold reserves which are still in Canada. [von Ribbentrop]

The reconstruction of Britain is to be undertaken commensurate with resources and at a pace in step with the reconstruction of the Fatherland. In accordance with the treaty leading to the cessation of hostilities [note not 'surrender'], Britain will be treated as if it were part of the Fatherland. The autonomous regions of England, Wales, Scotland, Northern Ireland and Southern Ireland will have the same structure and benefits as if they were part of Germany. Ireland was given the choice of joining in or staying out but actually had little choice as they would have presented a problem under the new regime and in particular the Kriegsmarine wanted their Atlantic coast. Autobahns are planned to connect major cities, the first ones radiating from Oxford. Priority is to connect the new capital with Cambridge which is becoming known as 'New Gottingen'. Volkswagen have taken over the motor plant in Birmingham, Auto Union are in Coventry and here in Oxford, Mercedes are setting up shop. The economy will soon recover under German management and with Swiss investment. Versprung durch Technik!

After concluding our first set of interviews, I asked him why they were all wearing traditional uniform instead of the Nazi style ones of the Third Reich? He responded with a smile that Churchill, in return for the repatriation of the British gold reserves, had insisted that there would be "No jackboots on British soil!"

[This concludes the first set of notes which I took in interview with Herr Rommel. I am invited to join him in Berlin at any time to take further notes and to meet with others who are not available in Oxford.]

PS - I hesitate to mention here one other point which occurred but which did not relate to the period that I was engaged to cover. I asked how Germany had managed to recover so quickly from the carnage of WWI and the serious debt that had been incurred during the period when the rest of the western world was mired in depression. His reply was cagey but I gleaned enough from it to come to my own conclusion. Which European country had the financial resources and a friendly population many of whom spoke the same language and had strong ethnic ties? However, I won't put this in the notes as Goebbels is bound to take it out. As partial confirmation of my theory, I later found out that the Isle of Man and the Channel Islands are to be made Cantons of Switzerland as some sort of reward for undefined services.

PPS – just found out – the 1948 Olympics are to be held in London!

13, T' Green
Old Great North Road
Balderton
Notts
1ˢᵗ April, 2010

Dear Mr Wogan

I understand that you are a broadcaster of some repute and have some considerable following amongst a certain faction of the population and this may have something to do with the events that befell me about this time last year.

[This story is a little long and I'm told that the attention span of your listeners is about 20 seconds so you may wish to split it into episodes.]

As I began - about this time last year I was abroad early one morning - walking the whippet - when I was accosted by a strange man who appeared to be hopping a large balloon, in a northerly direction, along the Old Great North Road. He stopped and tethered the balloon to a lamppost opposite my abode and asked "Do you know the way to Stan Drew's?" and as that's my name I answered in the affirmative, whereupon he grasped me by the hand and exclaimed loudly (in a false Scottish accent) that it was a wee further south than he had thought.

He then asked if I knew where 13, The Green was (he actually said "Where's the thirteenth green?") and when I pointed to my house he appeared a little puzzled. He then studied my lawn - it's a little large actually as I bought the pit site at the end of the terrace when it closed down. When he spotted my humble putting green he whooped with elation, knelt and kissed the turf. I've seen the Pope do this and thought that it must have had some religious significance.

He then proceeded to call someone on one of those new fangled mobly phones with no wires and within minutes we were inundated with rusty orange Volvo 340's all loaded to the gunwales with cheery old folks who greeted me as if I had taken them to the promised land.

They unloaded tents and marquees and stalls and all sorts of things from their car boots and for a while I thought they were going to hold a car boot sale on my lawn! Anyway they were fairly well behaved and even started put up AA road signs with strange writings on them such as "TOGS this way" and such. It meant nothing to me but soon over 5,000 people were all over my lawn and enjoying themselves - the local police were out directing traffic and everyone was having a whale of a time.

I was quite worried about damage to my lawn and all those people using my humble loo but the guy from Stannah Stairlifts gave me £500 to put up his tent and the lady from SAGA Holidays gave me even more for a good pitch.

Anyway all good things come to end and they were all terribly well behaved, setting off by eight o'clock to get home before dark. The guy with the balloon was last to go (Mr Gofar I think his name was) and he thanked me profusely for a lovely day. Unfortunately he failed to leave his address so I'll pass on the Chief Constable's good wishes for you to deal with - it's just a little note about the traffic jams.

Many happy returns to the TOGS who stopped off.

Stan Drew

Enclosed - Invoice from Nottingham Police for the use of Police Helicopter on traffic control in the sum of £4,317.19 +VAT

MONKY BUSINESS   BY PERCY VERANCE

A monastery, remote in the Himalayas, had only the nearby village to support it. Being so high up, there was nowhere to grow crops, and the only domestic animals able to stand the bleak winter were the yaks with their thick black woolly coats. However the hundred or so monks were ably supported by the small number of local villagers who brought food up the mountain from the low lands where crops could be grown. It was a hard life and, other than tending the yaks, there was little else to do for them other than to transport whatever was given to the monastery by donors from across the world. Generations had performed this duty admirably for several hundred years enabling the monks to concentrate on their prayers and meditation as they sought release from the cycle of reincarnation and admittance to the state of Nirvana.

My humble understanding of the way it works is that good things are taken into account in some sort of credit score and bad things incur debt. Any credit or debit is carried over to your next life which is part of a series of cycles which all souls have to undergo until they reach perfection and then achieve moksha - the state of nirvana at which point they no longer reincarnate.

Some versions of the religion, which I don't support, have added detail to the cycle of reincarnation arguing the thieves return as animals such as goats', murderers as snakes and wife beaters as rats (excuse me if the details are incorrect as they vary and appear to have no basis in the fundamental writings of the ancients on which most religion is based).

Thus life for the monks was an endless cycle of prayer and meditation interspersed with occasional relaxation in the form of making coloured designs which were assembled, in great detail, from dyed calcite which was laboriously gathered and ground up by hand. On completion these 'sand mandalas' were swept up and the minerals, which had gone into their production, ceremoniously returned to a stream in the mountains. Repetition and the undertaking of mundane tasks enabled the monks to concentrate their every thought on the meaning of life and how they would end the cycle which every human has to endure before their soul can cease to be reborn in the physical world. The premise is that there can be no higher aim in life and their removal from the real world below, and its endless tasks, provides the ideal path to enlightenment.

But then, without warning, disaster struck and the whole area was devastated after a small earthquake triggered an enormous landslide which buried both the monastery and the village. Only two small boys who were tending the yaks in their pasture were spared and after rescue, the pair were taken down the mountain leaving the animals to fend for themselves.

An Indian holy man – a Fakir - who lived nearby was reputed to be in contact with the afterlife and when consulted, and suitably rewarded, he deigned to give news about the spirits of those who had perished in the disaster. He was quite clear that the souls of the departed villagers, who had so tirelessly supported not only themselves but the monastery as well............

[At this point you are expecting a punch line to wrap up the story and, to be honest, Percy did write one but Pyotr decided not to use it at the editing stage. Having left enough clues, we're sure you can make up your own?]

A NOD AND A WINK   BY BERNADETTE NUNN

Let me introduce myself – I'm Sister Bernadette - a thoroughly modern nun with a degree in geography and medieval languages. As part of the Church's new approach to the modern world, I was recruited to the convent through their graduate development programme. I was nearing the end of my industrial experience year when they asked me to act as personal assistant to the Mother Superior for six months. Many think she is a dragon and out of place in a convent but after just a few days I found working for her is the best job in the world.

Let me explain that 'MS', as we call her, is one of the new breed of 'managers' within the Church – appointed to improve the running of the establishments such as convents and monasteries and make them self sufficient, just as when they were centres of industry, learning and commerce in the middle ages; before they were destroyed by Henry the Vandal and his hatchetman Thomas Cromwell.

Our business plan shows that we will cease to be a drain on central resources and become a net contributor in two years time. The governors thought this would be beyond the skills of any mere nun and wanted to bring in a professional manager but they did not count on the attributes of our MS. That's not to say that she hasn't had her problems with the more conservative characters who previously ran the establishment. With the attached girls' day school – our main source of revenue – she has responsibility for nearly five hundred faithful souls.

They say she has an MBA from Harvard but when Father O'Gill asked her to produce the certificate for his records she refused and made him take her word that she was qualified. Those who witnessed this confrontation said she stood up to him as if it were a test of wills between two stags in the rut and she, the stronger, prevailed. Since then they have not been the closest of friends and some say that Father O'Gill often seeks to undermine her authority. Of course as the only 'man' in the establishment he expects to prevail but in his confrontations with MS this is not the case.

So on my first day she had briefed me on my new role – the first time that such an appointment had been tried out in the convent. She said that I would be her representative, her eyes and ears, in the community and it was my job to know everything that was going on. I would also troubleshoot any minor matters which arose.

So I entered her study on the third day of my new job with some trepidation. She was sitting at her desk reading a letter written by Father O'Gill that had just been published in The Times. It was a response to an article on the previous day about a vicar who had changed sex. The Father's letter was a diatribe against the relaxation of standards in the faith and finished with a damning condemnation of the transgendered.

Without acknowledging my presence, MS got up from her desk and walked to the large bow window which looked out over the immaculate gardens and playing fields of the school. Ours is not an establishment to compromise on standards and the immaculate lawns and well tended vegetable gardens were a tribute to the improvements she had wrought at the school which was now the envy of many. Our waiting list of girls wanting to get in is the highest in the country for a single-sex denominational school.

As she looked out, I thought I heard her mutter a quotation from history. It was something like "Who will rid me of this troublesome priest?" But she had spoken it in ancient French and I corrected her use of the male pronoun as that language was my specialty during my outplacement in France. She sounded quite exasperated and I continued by asking her if she was addressing me but she responded that it was just a quotation from history and I should pay no heed.

"But what brings you to me at this time, my child?" she enquired in the practised tones that she reserved for her closest allies.

I brought myself back to the immediate task and blurted out "It's the Sixth Form, Mother, They're playing Russian Roulette!"

"Mother of God," she gasped and her voice dropped at least two octaves as it did when she was stressed. "Where are they getting the guns and ammunition – has anyone been hurt?"

I realised at once that my incomplete statement had been totally misleading and engendered an equally inappropriate reaction. I calmed down and set about a more measured and meaningful explanation.

"No Mother, it's to do with the inspection after morning assembly."

She interjected "If you mean the knickers inspection please say so."

I continued "Some of the fourth form started gambling by wearing forbidden underwear and it has now spread to the whole school. When the form number is drawn, to select the form for the day's inspection, there are six forms so the odds are the same as they are in Russian Roulette that you will be in the unlucky year that is selected. It came to a head yesterday when Sister Claire saw one of the girls having some form of religious seizure when the number was called out. At least she thought it must be religious as the girl was calling out 'Oh God, Oh God'.

"What should we do Mother? – It's rumoured that most of the senior school are wearing thin nylon things with lace and all sorts that should never grace an establishment like ours. Some have even been in to town to a shop called Ann Summers." I finished breathlessly.

"Wait my pet," she said, "we should not jump into an inappropriate response here – every cloud has its silver lining and one thing they taught me at Harvard is that every threat has an opportunity." She had not taken me into her confidence like this before and I sat silently for a full five minutes before she responded.

As she issued her instructions, she would write short notes to those concerned, confirming her orders. There never was a woman like this before – it was like being with a great general before a battle!

"Tell Sister Claire to call a special assembly at one o'clock in the main hall but not to inform any of the girls in advance. The whole school will undergo inspection before they leave the hall."

"But who will undertake the inspections?" I questioned – "Sister Mary is away in London and you have the teleconference with the Cardinal in Madrid at that time?" She was very much into this kind of meeting as she never travelled abroad. She said it was through fear of flying but I knew that it was because she did not possess a current passport and she refused to apply for new one as she did not have a photograph to attach to the application.

"Tell Father O'Gill that he will undertake the inspection." She continued baldly.

"But he's a man!" I stuttered, "and what if he refuses when I ask him?"

"Child," she responded, handing me the second note, "did I say 'ask him'? – I said 'tell him' that he is to undertake the inspection – was it not he, himself, who introduced the uniform rules five years ago? – as ye sow, so shall ye reap."

With that she gave me a single meaningful nod – just like Wellington giving his orders at Waterloo and I knew that this meant that the discussion was over. This was always her way of ending a discussion and dismissing you from her presence. I departed to do her bidding.

I entered the study as soon as she hung up from the teleconference.

"Mother Superior, something terrible has happened – Father O'Gill collapsed during the inspection and has been taken to hospital – they will ring you as soon as there is any news."

Ten minutes later it was confirmed that Father O'Gill had been pronounced dead on arrival, having suffered a massive heart attack.

The funeral was outstanding – Father O'Gill could not have done better if he had organised it himself. MS had taken charge herself and we had all excelled ourselves in making the service special.

The high spot was her delivery of the valediction from the pulpit – it was as if she were a general lauding the praises of her favourite lieutenant who had fallen in battle in the commission of a heroic deed! She was over-generous in her praise and in extolling the Father's (somewhat modest) achievements; praising his support for the traditional values of the church and glossing over his condemnations. She singled out his courage in continuing to work after his heart condition was diagnosed and his decision to keep the matter secret – sharing it only with her.

Being a 'member of staff' I was at the side of the nave, to provide support for the Mother herself, with one of the main pillars between me and the congregation. As she left the pulpit, to return to her seat, she turned away from those gathered to pay their respects and passed close by me. I could not be sure what it meant but as she passed by – and in my sight only – she smiled brilliantly and gave me an enormous wink!

THE LITTLE RED ENGINE   BY PYOTR

I was born in 1943, in the middle of WWII and I have often wondered how my parents could have been so careless to conceive me in the midst of all that conflict and at a time when the outcome was uncertain. To some extent, my mother answered that question, as she said, whenever I was naughty "I made a mistake." It was years later that I discovered what that meant when I came across cases of girls who were pregnant but not married. She also told me that she had considered an abortion but could not go through with it.

After the war was over, and we still had rationing, we moved to a brand new council house; it was 1947 I think. I have a clear memory of a day, just after moving, when my Uncle Alf came to visit us in Stourport where we had been evacuated to. After being demobbed from the Chindits, he had gone back to work at the Austin in Birmingham and, at that time car workers were amongst the best paid in the country. It was early in the day and my Dad was at work in Hartlebury at the RAF Maintenance Unit where he had worked since being bombed out of the BSA in Birmingham.

Alf and Mum talked about their experiences as if it was the first time they had met since the war began and he admired the new house. At Alf's suggestion, he walked me down to the town about a mile away. We went into the sweet shop on

Bridge Street and he bought me a small red dinky toy – a fire engine. I cherished it for years as it was the first real toy that I had. It's strange to remember things from so long ago but I have a clear recollection that I did not want the old style engine where the crew sat along either side of the engine on the outside; I wanted the more modern one with the flush front and the ladder on top.

As I grew up, my relatives from Birmingham were regular visitors. We lived (for them at least) 'in the country' and they were always made welcome by Mum and Dad. One of my lasting memories of those visits is how the conversation would often turn to the buses and where they ran. It was always a mark of someone who was savvy to know what number bus to catch and where to change to another. The names of Birmingham pubs often featured as landmarks and low-key arguments ensued about the best way to get from Erdington to Bearwood.

I had two sisters, the older being ten years senior than me and she 'mothered' me to a large extent, though, on one occasion, she did leave me outside the chemist' shop in my pram and had to go back to collect me. She married and left home when I was 10, which gave me a bedroom of my own. I had a happy childhood and made many friends on the council estate and later at school where I was considered quite academic. After A levels, I left home and went to University in Manchester which was a complete change. I experienced Chinese food and curries for the first time and, after graduation, which was problematical, I decided to stay and work in Manchester Town Hall. There was a lot for a young engineer to do as the slum clearance programme was in full swing and the new estates all needed to be designed and built.

I got married in 1968 and my Dad died on Christmas Eve in 69, just after we had moved into our first house which he never got to see. He had, however, seen his first grandchild, born to the younger of my sisters and absolutely doted on him. Our own children followed after we moved to Bury and we lived up north for some years before moving back south in the 70s.

Years went by and my mother moved from the council house which was too big for her on her own. She went into sheltered accommodation and eventually went into a care home after having both hips replaced. It was a downward spiral. I used to go down and visit, taking the youngest of our three boys with me. After the visit, as a reward for keeping me company, he played *Outrun* in the arcade on Bridge Street and I indulged in *Operation Wolf*.

On the last visit and just before she died Mum told me…."I know something about you that nobody else knows." I was just leaving and told her that I would like to hear what it was on my next visit. She died, peacefully in her sleep a few days later and I never got to ask her what it was that she wanted to tell me.

Years went by and, for some unknown reason, I relayed this exchange to my older sister who immediately replied "Perhaps she was going to tell you that you weren't your Dad's."

Almost without thinking, I replied "But that can't be right – I look like him and I have the family nose."

She didn't reply and a month later, as I was flying to South America, she passed away. So I never got to follow up on it.

Some time later I was set to wondering why she had said what she said and it puzzled me why she would have said it if it were not true. My Dad was one of ten and he had seven brothers – three of them had the distinctive family nose.

Mum disliked Joseph and Richard was a pure Christian who would never betray his wife, but what of Alf? During the war he was demoted after abandoning a military prisoner who he was escorting to Williton Barracks. This happened when he got word that his wife was being unfaithful and he was very cut up about it. I looked back at the evidence:

When Richard died it was Alf who came to deliver the news and Dad died the day after. My younger sister said it was the shock of losing a younger brother who he was very close to.

When my younger sister married, Alf took a great deal of interest in me as I was paying great attention to one of the bridesmaids. He told us that we would be next and he was right. Alf sang at our wedding and bought us a very nice present. He had married again and his second wife, Hilda was very attentive. Each time we met she would be effusive about us coming to visit them at home in Rubery. Did she know something?

When Alf died we were living in Coventry but my mother insisted that I take her to the funeral in Bromsgrove despite other family members being able and more conveniently placed. She was most insistent and brooked no argument so we went together. Did she have an agenda?

So, I cast mind back to the day he visited us in Stourport just after the war and that he had not stayed until Dad got home. I knew that Alf had served with The Chindits in WWII; he gave me his distinctive slouch hat, so he was in Burma for the latter half of the war – but where was he in 1942? His war service record confirmed that he was in England and joined Wingate's troop later in the year.

All of those who might know the truth are now dead so I just have to wonder. After discovering his wife's infidelity, did he visit Stourport and make love with my Mum while Dad was at work? I Guess I will never know the truth but, either way, he was my favourite Uncle and I still remember the little red engine with great fondness.

THE IMMACULATE CONCEPTION   BY SHIRLEY KNOTT

Abigail knew that it was going to be bad news as soon as she saw the expression on the specialist's face. However the consultant wrapped it up in such a way that Tony did not actually twig that their problem was all down to him and the cancer that was killing him. They made only tentative arrangements for their next consultation in order to give them time to decide what to do but she was already sure that they would not go down the route followed by so many with infertility problems. Their friends, John and Gill had spent years, and tens of thousands of pounds delving in procedures to maximise their chances of conceiving and all to no avail.

A plan started to form in her mind after spending a girls' night out in Leeds – a very special night when they had gone to see the renowned Chipmunks at the biggest night club in town. She had been struck by the likeness of the blond, Antonio, to her partner and had joined his on-line fan club in order to keep track of him. She worked out the rest of their UK tour and secretly penciled their dates into her diary. Alone, she went to two of their other dates in order to be sure of their performance and ascertained that Antonio always performed the penultimate act – live sex with a volunteer from the audience!

By the third performance she had ascertained that it was indeed an act – the girl chosen was a professional who was strategically situated and identifiable by her dress. She would be 'selected' in the same manner as the one chosen to sing *Can't live Without You* in a Barry Manilow concert. They even played it whilst the selectors toured the audience giving the impression that they were looking for a girl at random. She now knew different.

Marking up the calendar with their tour dates she compared them with her predicted bio rhythms which had been prepared for the fertility specialist. And Bingo! No, not bingo at all – there would be a match next month when the Chipmunks played Sheffield. She set about her preparations and made sure that she had an alibi well in advance so that there would be no awkward explanations with Tony.

On the night she turned up well in advance at the venue and parked where she would have a clear view of the stage door. The Chipmunks had gone inside but it was someone else that she awaited. Not long before the performance was due to start she saw her target; an attractive girl in her early thirties in a short skirt and stilettos. She jumped out of the car and managed to intercept her before she entered the venue and persuaded her to talk in the car for a few minutes. In this short time she got her to agree to be absent. She was to make a call to the venue and tell them that she was ill but had sent a substitute. The key identifier on this occasion was a red sash which she handed over in exchange for her fee.

Abigail was excited; not only was she to perform but she hoped the outcome would be the much more. She went in tingling all over.

Having a ticket at the end of a row, half way back in the stalls, she noted that this was usually where the 'volunteer' came from. She also perceived that one of the bouncers noted her red sash.

"Where's Josie?" he whispered as she went past.

"Sick," she replied and took her place in the stalls.

When *Can't Live Without You* started up she stood with all the other girls who were anxious to perform and she was relieved when Antonio had come onto the stage for this part of the performance. The bouncer dutifully selected Abigail 'at random' and conducted her to the stage. After a few short words with Antonio and giving her name as 'Josie', Antonio lead her to the couch which was centre stage in subdued light behind a muslin curtain which hid nothing but made their image to the audience softer and more romantic.

Antonio kissed her and held her whilst she responded enthusiastically. As they petted in anticipation of what was to come, he quietly complimented her as he removed her dress and scented her perfume. After a short while he laid her back on the couch to calls of encouragement from the audience and made a play of entering her. After a few false plays he did indeed mount her and she played her part admirably by crying out with pleasure. Being the true performer that he was, Antonio strung out their pleasure until she was gasping for him to come. The audience sensing this urged him on and he came all at once whilst she arched her back in ecstasy. As it was all over, Abigail gathered her clothes in order to leave as quickly as she could but she had to wait until the compere called the couple together.

To a thunderous ovation he extolled "…and what an immaculate performance from our volunteer, Josie!" She left by the stage door and got into her car which was parked outside. Once inside she lay along the back seat with her legs up on the back shelf for the next ten minutes and only got back upright when the club started to empty. She was ecstatic during the drive back home but had she succeeded?

Tony succumbed to his cancer a month before their son was born.

Ten years later she was telling her son about the birds and the bees, a parent-to-child talk about puberty and sex but he had already gleaned most of it from his friends at school. He wanted to know more about his father and how he came into the world.

"Do you remember the day you made me?" he questioned.

"Absolutely," she responded.

"….and what was it like?" he said.

She paused wistfully for a while and remembering the compere's words she said "Immaculate!"

THE LETTERS   BY SHIRLEY KNOTT

It was the week before Christmas and Jay was watching the local news on television - a spokesman for the Post Office was complaining about the amount of undeliverable mail. After a short speech concerning the non-use of postcodes he mounted a tirade against poor handwriting. When interrupted by the presenter, he held out an example to illustrate his problem.

"Just look at this," he said, holding out an envelope which appeared, from a distance, to be stamped and addressed in the normal fashion. Closer examination revealed that whilst the stamp was an ordinary first class one, the writing was unintelligible. It consisted of a regular, rounded scrawl that had the appearance of an address but made no sense as it was not real writing.

"We have targets for successful delivery and any like this have to be passed on to our 'undeliverable' section. They've been complaining about the number of items which are turning up in my area and have asked me to take measures to cut down on it. I'm completely stumped over what to do so I'm appealing to your viewers to help me over this one."

After the Christmas rush was over, Jay went along to the local sorting office and asked for the manager who had made the plea on television. He presented his card which showed his profession as Dr Wilson A Pickett, Psychological Profiler. The guy on the desk took it away and a few minutes later, he was invited into the manager's office.

After a few pleasantries and comments on the recent snow, the manager handed over two almost identical letters. Both had a valid stamp and were in the same regimented, unreadable hand. Neither had been opened. Jay took the two letters and as he examined them, the postal official proceeded to tell him that he thought profiling was a load of rubbish which made good television but was not much use in the real world. Jay proceeded to show the official how wrong he was.

"The writer of these letters," he commenced, "appears to be a lady who is rather shy. She's about 5'9" tall and likes to wear heels. Her bust is a 38 or 40c and she wears quite sexy, often black underwear. She is well made up, always goes out in skirts or dresses rather than trousers and posts her letters after dark. She uses Ebay quite a lot and may well be married but she's certainly not a lesbian."

He gaped open mouthed at the statement - "You'll be telling me next what she does for a living."

Jay handled one of the letters again and paused thoughtfully, "She's likely an engineer, ex-military or a lorry driver, probably likes steam trains," he said firmly.

"How can you possibly know what she does just for a living just from that scrawl on the letter – are you a handwriting expert as well?" he said.

"Well," he responded, "my conclusions are not based on that – rather on an analysis of who would want to post such a letter. Let me explain. First we have to look for the motivation – most people would assume that someone posting a letter would be wishing to communicate with someone else via that medium but what if the purpose is not that? What if our correspondent just wishes to appear to be posting a letter, late at night?"

"But why would a lady wish to do that?" he asked.

"Did I say it was a lady? Actually, I said she appears to be a lady and that gives the game away. Our letter writer is a closet transvestite who goes out after dark and takes a dummy letter with her so that any of the neighbours who see her assume that she is posting it and that's why she is out so late. If we see someone with a purpose we are less likely to query other aspects such as their appearance. Many transvestites appear to be from the occupations I mentioned and the other attributes are just those which could apply to any typical TV."

"So how do I solve the problem," he asked. "Knowing what is going on does nothing to prevent it happening. How do I find out where the letters are coming from?"

"I already told you that. 'She' uses Ebay a lot and will have lots of small soft packages delivered via the mail. This is the most likely way 'she', being a closet tranny, buys her clothing especially underwear. This will focus on a small number of customers in the immediate area and once identified we can probably reduce the sample down to one or two by looking out for certain items in the post. Once you have found the possible source, just return one of the letters, with the normal mail and the problem should go away."

A week later, Jay returned to the office to find out if the problem had been solved.

"Wow," said the manager, "I take back all I said about profiling. I already have an idea who we might be dealing with. Thank you so much Dr Pickett, but haven't I heard your name somewhere before?"

"Yep," Jay responded, "I just borrowed it from someone on the television and printed some cards on my computer at home."

"You mean you're not a trained profiler at all? I can't believe you could work out who it was and go into such detail – how did you know this was the work of a transvestite?"

"It takes one to know one." Jay said with a broad wink.

THE TOWER OF BABEL　　　　　BY PYOTR

There was time when I was young and impressionable when I was forced, under duress, to learn French. This was an essential component of the syllabus of the grammar school which I attended and a pass at 'O' level was a requirement for matriculation. The headmaster explained that learning French was a requirement in case I should become a diplomat as it was the 'lingua franca' of the foreign office. I scraped a pass on the third attempt and promptly gave up all interest having acquired a lasting distaste for anything Gallic. If I wanted to go to Oxford or Cambridge then I would have to get 'O' level Latin or Greek and, of course the Latin would be essential if I was considering medicine or pharmacology.

At college I discovered that most of those on engineering courses were learning German; or, at least, technical German. This would enable them to read scientific and technical papers which were frequently written in that language (we have many things to thank Max Planck and Albert Einstein for but this is not one of them).

Years later I went to work in Mexico and learnt (learned?) sufficient Spanish to converse with the taxi drivers. I frequently cursed the education system which had ignored this most elegant language which I found both interesting and useful. At this time one of my children had learned French and Latin and he was progressing well in Russian with a view to joining the armed forces who actually wanted him to learn Serbo-Croat. Obviously this requirement has been overtaken by the need for Arabic speakers.

"What a mess!" You may say but things have changed though my view of languages, with the exception of Spanish, has really not moved on. Interestingly, I often come across people who are astounded to find that Spanish is the primary language in many parts of the USA, especially Florida. What they fail to realise is that the state was purchased from Spain and that Spanish was the main language long before Americano (the version of English spoken across the pond) became favourite. Obviously French was (and still is) spoken in Louisiana which was acquired in a similar manner though I don't think that Alaska came with an indigenous Russian speaking population. Texas was also assimilated from Mexico after its war of independence and the other southern states came over (some say illegally) after the American-Mexican War and Santa Anna's capture. What's the relevance of this to our story? Well, one might argue, if things had happened in a different order, and Washington had been built in Florida, then Americans might all be speaking Spanish instead of Americano.

Where does this take us? Well (again), we now have a new lingua franca and one which covers all of the issues raised above and this is all down to *Murphy's Golden Rule*. This states that: 'the man with the gold makes the rules' – and who has the gold? – The USA so they decide what language we speak.

There are, however, several basic reasons why the world speaks English which relate to the motherland:
- The British Empire, now the Commonwealth
- Dickens and Shakespeare as representatives of English literature
- The BBC World Service

The rest all point to that version of English which is widely used by ex-colonists across the water and which can be listed as:
- Hollywood - through its endless outpourings of visual images and subsequently to *Friends* as epitomising the new generation
- Elvis - who made popular music a worldwide phenomena with the exception of the Soviet Union; we had to wait for The Beatles to break down the Iron Curtain
- Boeing – as the providers of cheap international travel; every international airport and carrier in the world uses English to inform passengers
- IBM/Microsoft - who brought computers into business and later into every home with the development of the PC and cheap software
- Coca Cola - who created a business with trademarks that are recognised across the world and made it cool to converse in English
- The Internet - which, despite being invented by a Brit, is almost a 100% American led development

There have been the occasional counter movements: in Israel where Hebrew was adopted as their national language on the achievement of their nationhood and in India where Indira

Gandhi threw out English and foolishly adopted Hindi as the national tongue – a decision still regretted across much of India with the notable exception of Delhi.

The American influences are the key issues in making English into the world's vocal exchange currency and this is now apparent in China where all children are learning it as their second language. I recently took out a bet over which country would be the first to ditch its national tongue and adopt English; Finland and Greenland were near the top of the list but a colleague tells me that it is already underway in Rwanda, much to the chagrin of the francophone minority and the Quay d'Orsay.

But English is not an easy language, you say? Well (again), it is easy to learn the basics but difficult to become fluent because of the peculiar spellings. I once took a visitor from India out for a meal on the Melton Road in Leicester. After the meal he told me that he had to get back to Lowburow. "Loughborough?" I said questioningly. "Yes Luffboruff," he responded.

So what should we do about our wonderful language? "Keep it the same as it's always been," comes the chorus of the ignorant and ill informed. But should we change it – the Americans have and generally for the better. Even the Oxford English Dictionary uses some of the changes as standard e.g. 'stigmatize' rather than 'stigmatise'. Language is never a dead thing; it is a living entity and moves with the times. Parents often have difficulty with the vocalisations (or vocalizations) of their children and most cannot understand the lyrics of a rap number.

My view is that we should, in collaboration with other English speaking nations, set up a system to simplify spelling and pronunciation changing, by agreement, about ten words each year starting with such obvious candidates as fight, might, sight, night and light. This development would be called *Standardized English* and become the way in which English is taught internationally. Those at home who wish to adopt it would be free to do so and those who don't could continue in the old ways until their version simply withers on the vine.

If <u>we</u> don't do it then someone else will!

BIRD SPOTTIN' BY ROBIN TWITCHER

> **I saw a buzzard floating high**
> **Upon the clouds he seemed to fly**
> **As if he'd taken drugs a mite**
> **He soared above – high as a kite!**

Actually, not many people can tell the difference between a buzzard and a kite. Some birds are very difficult to tell apart, for instance the raven and the carrion crow. Apparently the raven has a triangular tail whereas the crow has broader tail feathers – always stumps me.

But then the buzzard and kite are quite easy to tell apart. A buzzard is larger than a kestrel and smaller than an eagle; it has broad bird-of-prey wings and has light patches on its underside. A kite is very nearly identical but it has a long length of string attached with a small boy at the end of it.

> **A twitcher's book with names he'd brag**
> **The lowly cormorant or shag**
> **But tell the difference he could not**
> **His pristine scorecard he did blot!**

So how do we deal with this one? Well there a number of things to consider and firstly we must mention Austin Powers. When his first film was released in America they had to produce a short glossary as Yankee Doodle Dandy did not understand the words used in the home of our common tongue. But it's another one which is quite simple – if in doubt you don't get a cormorant on a Saturday night. So on the same theme you could just count the birds; one on its own would definitely be a cormorant (just like crows versus rooks) and if there are two and one is on the back of the other then it's definitely a shag. This is often a forerunner to nest building and egg laying.

> **Up in the air of any fowl**
> **I'm fondest of the tawny owl**
> **But when about or on a hike**
> **I do not like the murderous shrike**

Many birds have reputations to protect and the magpie is probably the clearest example:

"Good morning Mr Magpie, how's your wife?"

This is essential good manners if you want to avoid their bad books but being able to tell the sex of many birds is not so easy:

> **A martin passed by close to me**
> **But sex I know not – he or she?**
> **For parents we could not tell best**
> **As both of them attend the nest**

And many of the sayings are old wives' tales which refer to the weather:

A shag in the morning – shepherd's delight!

You couldn't say the same about a magpie but many birds can talk for themselves:

> **The swallows they went flying by**
> **And all who saw said 'my oh my'**
> **What lovely birds they are so cute**
> **And calling so, they are not mute**

But enough of these little birds; what of their grander cousins:

> **There was a swan that I saw swimmin**
> **It was admired by men and wimmin**
> **All white and feathered, quite renown**
> **Not dull and brown, a bird uptown**

But above all, you cannot ignore Robin Redbreast for his cheek:

> **I sat dockside awatching robin**
> **While all about the gulls were bobbin**
> **But little red breast set the trend**
> **No doubt that he, my honest friend**

Enough of this nonsense!

POINTS OF VIEW   BY JANE PETERS

THE FAMILY

"Come on mum, we'll be late for school."

"Jack, will you move your car, it's in the way and I can't get past it."

"Take mine; I'll use the Beamer for work."

"You know I can't drive it; it's such a beast and I can't reach the peddles."

"Just adjust the seat; it's really easy."

"Oh that electric thing just confuses me – OK, just this time."

THE HUSBAND AND WIFE

"Jack, now don't worry, the kids are fine it's just a little bump and those funny fangled bars at the front are a bit bent."

"What you bent my Machero? What happened?"

"Well you know how I have a problem reaching the peddles; well when I got to the end of Windlesham Avenue the car refused to stop and I ran into one of those little red things that a lot of the mums use. The ambulance driver was very nice and said that they should be OK but he wasn't sure about the little girl."

"Is it badly damaged? You managed to drive it home OK?"

"It's OK to drive as those bull bar things at the front took the impact and stopped us getting hurt; they did get rather badly bent though. I couldn't drive the car home so the police took it away and gave us a lift in a patrol car."

THE POLICE OFFICER

"At 08.28, this morning a black Machero collided with a red Quito at the junction of School Lane and Windlesham Avenue. The occupants of the smaller car were a local woman, aged 35 and her two children, a boy aged six and an eight year old girl. The boy suffered only minor injuries but the girl, who was on the side near to the collision, was taken to hospital with suspected concussion. The occupants of the larger vehicle were unharmed."

THE HOSPITAL ADMINISTRATOR

"At 08.59 this morning an eight year old girl was brought to the A&E department by ambulance following a collision between two vehicles. It is with regret that I have to inform you that she was pronounced dead on arrival at 09.05. The coroner has been informed and a police investigation is underway."

THE INSURANCE ADJUSTER

"We are in receipt of your claim in respect of the accident suffered by your wife on the 23rd of this month whilst driving your vehicle WHO11. Our loss adjuster has seen the vehicle, which was impounded by the police and has discovered that it is fitted with the old style 'bull bars'. Whilst these were legal when the car was new, the new regulations forbid them from being fitted to new cars from the 25th May. You are not in contravention of these new regulations, however, we wrote to you on the 21st January informing you that we would no longer cover any vehicle which continued to have them fitted. A copy of this letter is attached and you confirmed its receipt and content when you renewed your policy on the 2nd February.

I have to inform you, therefore, that your insurance policy is invalid and Big Boy Insurance will not be assuming liability for any claim resulting from use of the vehicle whilst the offending bars were fitted. Should you wish to contest this decision a copy of our complaints procedure is included with your policy document."

THE JUDGE

"I am required to take into account your admission of guilt in this matter and your obvious remorse for the harm that you, as a mother yourself, have caused to another family. But the seriousness of the outcome requires me, in addition to a lengthy driving ban, to include the minimal custodial sentence that is recommended for a conviction for causing death by dangerous driving…"

THE BANK MANAGER

"Well, Mr Forbes, it seems that things have really gotten out of hand. Obviously most claims of this nature are covered by motor insurance but I gather that yours was not valid. This brings us to the problem of how to resolve the claim for damages against you which, I have to say, is most substantial. You property is mortgaged to us and the equity, following deduction of the debt, will not be enough to cover the outstanding claim against you. We will, therefore, be foreclosing on the property at the end of the month."

THE CORONER

"We have no doubt that Jack Forbes took his own life as the manner in which he died leaves no doubt on that score and this is confirmed by the content of the letter that he left. Rarely have I come across such a sad train of events and looking back at the initial cause, which has left two families, each with a terrible loss, I must say that had he taken note of the requirement to amend the equipment on his vehicle, then none of this need have happened."

THE DIRECTOR OF SOCIAL SERVICES

"I can confirm that, following a request to attend at St Justin's Preparatory School this afternoon, two related children were taken into the Authority's care pending the release of their mother from prison on compassionate grounds."

ABOUT TIME　　　　　BY FELIX SCHRODINGER

Brian Greene waxed elegantly about it in; Julian Barbour said it didn't exist; Steven Hawking almost ignored it in a book that featured it in the title; Michio Kaku talked around it in four hours of television and Brian Cox admitted straight out he didn't know what it is. Perhaps only Fritjof Capra came near to the truth. It affects us all every minute of every day but how and why? Does it have a mechanism and can we ever hope to understand it?

Alongside this line of thought is an apparently unrelated topic. What is the vacuum energy and does it have a function? Everything in nature appears to be there for some reason. Is it possible that the vacuum energy is real but it has no purpose? Or is it just that we have not (yet) devoted enough attention to it in order to understand what it does?

Wave particle duality is quite well understood and one can take a simplistic view that matter moves as a wave and arrives as a particle hence the phenomena we call decoherence. This is a way of looking at the way that two particles are required to come into contact with each other in order to become part of the real world. They only do this when their combined probabilities exceed a critical value and they then become real rather than an ethereal wave. As described so clearly in Richard Feynman's elegant diagrams they are shown in two dimensions but what if a third ingredient is required in order for decoherence to take place?

Supposing that the sum of the probabilities of the two particles alone are not enough to bring about collapse of the wave function but a third element is required and that is supplied by the virtual particles which emanate from the vacuum? Instead of *P(a) + P(b)* we require *P(a) + P(b) + P(c)* to exceed the critical value where 'c' represents a particle appearing from the vacuum energy. As it has a rhythm which is time related itself, then we have a mechanism by which particles achieve a regulated motion.

Whether the appearance of virtual particles is random or has a pattern is, as yet, undiscovered but either way this would not affect our appreciation of time as a random pattern at the quantum scale would not be apparent to us. A potential link with consciousness can be drawn as our brains consist of particles which undergo this same process.

Currently the arrow of time is usually described as a result of entropy always increasing but it can be argued that this is an interesting effect rather than a fundamental cause.

What other effects might we see from this supposition? The explanation of matter clumping in the formation of galaxies and planets has always relied on the manufacture of gravitational models that are made to fit the outcome which, as we now see, does not always work; the current focus on dark matter being a case in point. If there are variations in the density of the vacuum energy then this would provide an underlying platform where matter particles would tend to decohere resulting in clumping.

Whether such variations are by accident or design is another point for consideration but it is a scenario which could also explain the property whereby virtually all celestial bodies spin.

MY MUSICAL FRIENDS — BY PYOTR

I hadn't realised until recently how privileged I was to have such special friends when I was growing up. Having been quite academic and tone deaf, I underestimated the talents of those close to me who could actually understand and even read music.

I remember one of the street parties which we used to have, after the war and into the 1950s, on any state occasion such as a coronation, royal wedding or jubilee. It's sad that times have moved on and they rarely happen now. Anyway, it was 1953 (I think) and we were all out in the street having consumed our jelly and blancmange, when Matt's dad wheeled out the piano. They were the only ones in the street to have one; an upright as our post-war council houses would not have had room for anything bigger. Once settled Matt placed some sheet music in place and commenced to play – *something street rag* I think it was but then who cares – we just wanted something to dance to and this was it. After a few minutes of energetic jigging around we found that we couldn't keep time with the music; all the notes were there and in the right order but there was no sense of rhythm, despite the tick-tock of a metronome on top of the piano. We concluded that, talented though he was, his music was not for us.

Tommy, my next door neighbour, was an outstanding soprano, as well as an accomplished footballer, who became the lead singer in one of our local rock bands which sprang up after the skiffle revolution. Remember this was pre-Beatles and buying a Fender Telecaster was a major investment. As I was the only one with a driving licence, and John was the only one with a car, we essentially became 'roadies' for a short time after the Crestas were formed. As the electric guitar revolution progressed, and more venues sought groups to perform, having transport was essential. You couldn't do gigs using the bus, especially if you were the drummer. The Crestas performed admirably for over twenty years before the gloss wore off and they disbanded.

Cliff lived at the other end of our close and was a year younger. He was actually writing songs in his early teens and also took on the role of lead singer in the other big group in town – the Cruisers. Whilst Tom had a passing resemblance to Tommy Steel, Cliff based his persona squarely on Elvis; even the hip swinging. The Cruisers also performed around the area for over twenty years before things tailed off and they broke up.

My other school friend, Terry lived in the main part of town and was also a talented soprano. His interest, after the death of Buddy Holly gravitated towards the classical side and so he never joined in the pop revolution; being part of the choir was his forte.

Finally, I have to say that it was a privilege to have been part of that scene and times which had a great impact on my life. Tommy became sales director of a manufacturing company;

Terry became managing director of a large carpet firm and Cliff, after teaching, went on to become a professional song writer with a number of special hits.

Oh, what of Matt, the talented pianist with no sense of rhythm? I lost touch with his career but someone told me that he became a famous modern jazz pianist.

GOBBOLINO THE WITCH'S CAT BY PYOTR

We have always had cats in the family and each one brought its own personality with it. Our first was a rescue cat, not from a sanctuary but actually caught off a factory rooftop and taken home. Snagglepuss certainly had personality. He wasn't a youngster but once he had settled down to domestic life and ready meals he became playful. When my wife sang *Beautiful Dreamer* he would join in between each line with a somewhat mournful 'meow' and if she then sat and ate a biscuit he would climb up her front and pat her face as she chewed. But his party trick came when he played in the garden chasing a curtain wire. When the game finished he would lead you back in to the first floor apartment from the garden with the end of the curtain wire in his mouth.

Daisy joined us soon after and we all thought that she was mad. We called her 'Daisy Drain' because, when it rained, she would sit on the window sill and chatter to the birds outside. Snowy and Smudge followed soon after we bought our first house and they had to be tamed as they had been born wild. Snowy would commute each day, across the field at the back of the house, to the abandoned reservoir site and hunt for mice; his sister Smudge would sit out back in the early evening and wait to greet him when he returned from work. He was our shortest lived cat after being hit by a car but Smudge became our longest lived of all at the age of seventeen.

The animal sanctuary, where we did some part time work had a problem cat who had been abandoned after suffering a serious injury. His right front leg was completely stiff and so he walked a little like a pirate with a wooden leg. We called him 'Alfred the Great' as he was the largest cat we ever had. About that time my wife gave up work to have children and we acquired a dog. I found her (the dog not the wife) in a field when looking for a manhole cover to locate the route of a sewer (main drainage was my specialty). When she first arrived she was so small that she could almost fit in a pint glass. Alfie and Honey would wrestle and the cat would nip her gently. But she grew and he didn't so when she was fully grown, she would sit on him and nip his legs while he wriggled helplessly on the floor.

In Coventry we had our second dog and he, Rusty, was absolutely dreadful but so lovable. If you have ever watched the film *Marley and Me* you will know what pains we went through. He loved to play Scalextric and rag wrestling with our oldest boy.

When Rusty died my wife rescued Sootica from a man at the vets who had taken her there to be put down. She was completely black so we thought of her as a witch's cat. Her party trick was to haul herself up to the table after Sunday Lunch by digging her claws into my leg as I sat at the table. I took to wearing thick jeans in expectation as otherwise it was quite painful. Sooty was also a sort-of watchdog. She liked to be out at night and woe betide any of the urban foxes which came into her territory.

At about that time we were reading a childrens' book to the youngest boy at bedtime – *Gobbolino the Witch's Cat* which featured a black cat called Sootica and it became a family favourite. So, when after a big family barbeque the previous night, I found a small black and white cat asleep on the charcoal bag next morning it was fated that she would become Gobbolino. She was small, mostly black with some white patches, mute but would come when you whistled. We suspected that she had arrived in my brother-in-law's car from Worcester but after making enquiries, to no avail, we adopted her – a 'walk in' off the street.

She had lovely soft fur and was just like a 'rag doll' to handle. The boys would stuff her up their shirt and walk round with her head sticking out between the buttons. She never complained and was always up for a game. Her favourite was to play 'snakey'. I would confront her on the stairs and make a cobra shape with my arm and hand which she would attack vigorously. She was, however, such a wimp that even her most vicious assaults did not hurt; only once did she ever draw blood and that was by mistake.

All of our animals have been loved but when Gobbo died, from a thrombus, I was heartbroken. I still grieve whenever I think about her and the unconditional love that she gave me. A true soul mate who I look forward to being with in Heaven.

But now my grandchildren are reading the book; *Gobbolino the Witch's Cat* will never be forgotten.

LURNING INGLISH ANON

Elssware in this anthology, I rote abowt how and wy Inglish had becum the 'Lingua Franka' ov thu wurld. Itz sed that Inglish iz an eezy langwidge tu lurn badly butt won ov thu most diffikult tu lurn well. Ennyway, itz poppularity iz nott based on that butt on itz wydespred usidge espeshially in relashun tu Amerika and itz kulchur. Bering in mynd that most lurnerz just want tu speke it wy du they hav tu restul with ower inkonsistent spelling? If wee had an eezy tu lurn alturnativ wud that not bee ov grayt valyu?

Well, yu say, wee alreddy hav fonetiks and foniks, whatever they ar so wy du wee need a new won? Actchully they av been tryde as a method ov teeching in skule but thee eggsperryment waz abandund yurs ago and wee reverted tu tradishunal methuds.

Kan yu immagin how wunderful it wud bee if thoze lurning the langwidge wur alwayze prezented with konsisstant spelling? Wylst they wud hav problems with reding normal Inglish, for a wyle, aktchully it wud bee no diffurunt to uss wen wi try to rede Shakespeare or evun Chaucer. Thiss iz a ryme witch I liked befor wee had politikal korrectness:

> **There woz a yung kweer from Kartume**
> **Tuck a lezbianne up tu hiz rume**
> **They argyude orl nyte**

Abowt hoo hadd thu ryte
Tu du wot and with witch and tu hoome

Eethur way, I am kondukting a lobbying kampane ov Parlermunt tu try and get this aksepted and invyte yu tu joyn mee in thiss effurt.

I wud lyke tu ryte mor butt thu spell chekker iz full and it woent let mi du enny mor.

Appollogees if I hav spelt ennything rong.

BLENDING IN   BY LEE FRAKE

Jack was always one to investigate his new environment thoroughly. As soon as he had settled into the hotel room he set off to find the bar and to sample the local beer. He had heard that Bangalore was the Burton-on-Trent of India but instead of the relative cool of the Deccan he was five hundred miles away on the Corromandel coast. Either way it was the same beer, Golden Eagle they called it, and instead of those stupid little bottles they use in Singapore these were man sized - the old imperial pint and a quarter the barman had told him.

He sank a couple and then asked for the bar phone to see if the rest of the gang were alive or crashed out with jet lag. Strangely, flying economy had caused him less problems than he had thought. Obviously he had missed the comfort of the bigger club class seat but the company on the Air India flight and their abstinence had caused him to imbibe less. "Jet lag is caused 40% by waiting about in airports, 20% by flying and 40% by the amount of booze you consume" thus spoke Alfred, his long time friend and mentor.

Either way his mates who had flown club were not in evidence. He decided to explore the hotel and soon found himself outside admiring the pool. It used to be the biggest in the city and had been constructed with the hotel around on four sides. Completed in 1930, and hardly altered since - at least externally - the hotel was a classic example of British Raj architecture. He could almost smell the G'n'T from over the years. Once _the_ place to stay it was now by-passed by the wealthy who resided instead at the Sheraton or the Hiatt. These newer hotels were built to purpose with windows that had a view - not the poky little ones, designed before air conditioning, to let little light and hence heat in.

Jack found himself lounging beside the pool and admiring its symmetry - a perfect rectangle set in the equally perfect rectangle of the hotel building, palm trees down both long sides and bougainvillea draped canopies at either end. A small squirrel with yellow stripes on its back was making a din at a mynah bird that had dared settle on the bougainvillea - the squirrel's preserve. Overhead he noticed the kites soaring in the thermals and wondered why he had spent a whole weekend in Wales just looking at them - they were as common as sparrows here.

Everything was interesting and, on the way from the airport, he had soaked in the noise, the smells, the heat, the poverty and the pure vibrancy of the light. Not everyone could take the extremes that the sub-continent hit you with - culture shock they called it - but environment shock might be more appropriate.

Jack had no such problems; he had worked in Kenya, in Mexico, Nepal, Hong Kong and The States - all to great effect with much credit to his name. His creed was to look carefully at his environment and to blend - not to conflict. Much of his success was due to his ability to adapt to the people around him. In overseas work the failure rate is high - 50% for new initiates. Illness, home sickness, incompetence, inability to adapt, alcoholism, divorce and infidelity - he had seen them all and experienced some.

He sat by the pool in the late afternoon sun and watched a painter sprucing up the markings around the pool. The painter was using a bright red paint to go over the depth markers on the pool side and he noted how the paint dried within seconds. He also noted that the deep end was just deep enough to dive though there was no board, '6-6' it said and '2-0' at the other end. At six foot four and ninety five kilos he made a fair splash when he went in. Save it for when it's cooler he thought and started to address the project notes he had brought out. Soon he moved to the shade as his African tan had faded a little and he disliked the inconvenience of sunburn - it held up your development of a full blown tan.

After the beer he was gratified, as he thought about the sub-continent and its common preoccupation with cricket. After his work and real ale this was his greatest interest in life. In between playing he had become a guru on the facts of the game and since giving up playing had become a member at Edgbaston. At college he read Wisden as much as his engineering course not that that had stopped him getting a doctorate in his specialty - the natural treatment of industrial wastes.

The next day he continued to work on his tan, a labour of love and a precise task not to be rushed. He had a complex skin condition which gave him an allergy to water on his face so he never shaved; thus he sported a full set of dark curly whiskers which tended to offset his black thinning hair on top. There was ne'er a trace of grey atop his six foot four frame.

Frank was out on a twelve month secondment, after having marital issues – one of those abroad because of the problems at home. He was frequently alone when other team members were not present so had built up a routine which suited him. Besides swimming every day – he was an excellent swimmer - he arranged to eat every evening, outside of the monsoon season, at the poolside and the staff set up a table to suit whatever number of the team was present. There were several newbies tonight; two of them had 'Nehru' style suits made at a local tailors' and decided to wear them. There was building work going on at the hotel and this conflicted with the poolside so Frank's normal table was switched, at short notice, to the opposite side of the pool from where it was normally. No problem you would think in a perfectly symmetrical setup.

After consuming a great selection of barbequed tandoori style food, served at the poolside, everyone was in great mood and the Golden Eagles were going down fast; followed by even a few chasers. But the heat was still oppressive and obviously, there was no air conditioning at the poolside. All of a sudden Jack jumped up and shouted, "Who's for a swim?" at which point he took off and dived fully clothed, into the pool. However, not having taken note of the building works, he was unaware that the table had been set up on the opposite side of the pool. Thus his full 95kg and 6' 4" frame entered the pool at the shallow end!

Seconds later he emerged from the water with blood streaming from his scalp. "Help me! Oh f****** help me!" he called in panic. Two colleagues immediately entered the pool and helped him out laying him down on the poolside. Hotel staff were quick to respond and immediately controlled the bleed but it was obvious that hospital treatment was required. Accompanied by Frank, he was soon en route in a taxi which took them, post haste, to the nearby hospital with emergency facilities. Suffice to say that he survived the ordeal and, after an X Ray, which confirmed no permanent damage, he was stitched up and discharged with a large bandage covering his scalp and down under his chin to keep it secure. It looked a little like a turban but not so elegant.

Over the next week he was not able to work so spent much of his time relaxing by the pool; his tan was now even and getting darker by the day. Having been aware for some time that the next test match was to take place in the city, he was eagerly awaiting the arrival of the South African team who he held in great esteem. His favourite cricketer of all time was the great all rounder Hansie Stellenbosch and he wondered if it was possible to meet with him. After a few phone calls and some beneficial interference from the hotel manager, he ascertained that Hansie, having been engaged in an IPL Twenty 20 match, was to travel separately from the rest of the team and would arrive at the airport the following day. The team manager, being preoccupied with other matters, readily agreed that Jack could pick him up and provide transport to the team hotel.

Jack determined the arrival time of the flight and got to the airport an hour early to be sure that he could greet his idol. He had a white card marked with Hansie's name and, with his tan and 'turban', most thought he was a local taxi driver picking someone up. The plane landed and he waited patiently for his esteemed guest to clear baggage collection and customs. At last his guest appeared and Jack held up the card with his name on it which was instantly recognised.

Hansie walked across and simply deposited his bags on the floor in front of Jack who had to follow with them as Hansie walked off to the exit.

As he departed, with a crestfallen admirer trailing behind, he was observed to make a remark under his breath. It might have been something like "F****** Kaffers**…..can't get away from them these days!"

Note: * = u, * = c, * = k, * = i, * = n, * = g.

** Africaans for 'W**s'

A SUITABLE CASE FOR TREATMENT   BY AVRIL ENGANES

It was all the rage in the 90s – early retirement. Many of the privatised industries saw the future in new technology which meant downsizing of the workforce. Thus regular leaving-do's were held and many a gold watch presented (actually not so much of the gold – more Rotary than Rolex).

"Hi Barry," said The Chief Executive as he entered the washroom and opened his flies for a pee "are you doing Foster' today or is it me?"

"Yes, it's me unfortunately," said The Managing Director in response "but you can have him if you want – he's always been a bit problematical and you've known him as long as I have. He's here already – just met him coming out as I came in. Remember that time when he did the April fool in the paper about the tea bag mountain at Stoke Bardolph?"

Foster had been pictured alongside a large pile of compost which appeared to be tea bags. The article appealed to residents not to dispose of tea via the sink as it was blocking up the detritors and hence the work's treatment process.

"Can't say I appreciate actions like that," he continued, "but most of the staff thought it a great hoot and it exposed our human side to some benefit with the public."

"Yes, I remember and no, I'll delegate." said the Chief Executive turning to face the Managing Director. "What did he choose for his leaving present – something weird, I bet?"

"Yes," replied the MD, "a set of jewelers' drills with very fine bits which can drill down to a tenth of a millimeter." He said drawing up his zip and then exclaimed in amazement: "What on Earth have you done?" He was looking at the Chief Executive's groin which exhibited a large wet patch in the place around the zip as if you hadn't finished peeing properly.

The CE examined his saturated trousers and looked back at the Managing Director who exhibited a similar patch at the very same place.

"You too! What's going on?"

They turned to the taps and turned one on; as they looked closely, they could see a fine jet of water squirted out at exactly at the right angle to wet the hand washer's groin.

"Foster!" they exclaimed in unison.

He had to settle for the manager at the sewage treatment plant for his leaving presentation.

APRIL, A YEAR LATER.

"What's this?" said The Chief Executive, "another bloody jape by that clown. We should have kept him; at least we could control him then. But now he's a completely loose cannon – what are you going to do about it?"

"I'm inclined to think – nothing." replied the MD. "If we are seen to take it seriously then we could be ridiculed. Let's just ignore it and see what happens."

They were referring to a newspaper article in the *Nottingham Post* which featured a picture of Foster on the bank of the River Trent near the outfall from the sewage treatment plant. He was holding a dead fish (which he'd bought that morning from a local fishmonger) and the article went on to explain that fish were dying because of the ammonia content of the effluent from the plant. The Environment Agency had requested a further stage of treatment but the water company had declined on the basis that it would cost over ten million pounds and it was not good value for their customers to invest so much for so little benefit. The Managing Director, himself, had gone on Midlands Today to explain the problem and why they were not taking action.

Now, Foster, in the article, was suggesting a novel way to bring about an improvement for the reduction in the pollutant, the primary source of which is urine. He was proposing a trial whereby all men, above the age of ten, would urinate on their back lawns instead of using the normal bathroom facility. As well as reducing the ammonia loading it would also save water. The trial was to run for a month starting today – April 1st.

A MONTH LATER

"Sir – it's Mrs Waters from the Agency and she wants to talk urgently, I know you said you didn't want your meeting with the other directors interrupted but shall I put her through?"

"It would seem to be relevant to our discussions so please do." replied the Chief Executive.

"Hello, Virginia, how are you?" said the CE in a completely false tone as they had not been anything like cordial since the split up of the operating company and the regulator." He was also somewhat envious that she had been named after the most expensive postcode in the country.

"What?" he exclaimed after a short pause. "Well, if that's what you want we'll see what we can do."

With that he put the phone down and then discussed the issue with the assembled director and managers. According the Agency's monitors, the ammonia levels in the river had dropped 37% since the trial began and the river water was almost acceptable for the fish. A similar improvement in the discharge would mean that the river would achieve its targeted standard without the need for the major plant improvements. They agreed to extend the scope of the trial and let it run for another two months.

As everyone left the meeting the CE turning to the MD and, recalling how the situation had come about, said:

"Oh, Barry, will you ask Foster to drop by and let us know if he has any ideas on how we are going to break this to the ladies?"

THE ROAD TO DAMASCUS BY PYOTR

After the war, I grew up on a council estate in a small village across the River Severn from the canal town of Stourport which had been our home following the family's evacuation from Birmingham during the war. I attended a church junior school, which, considering its lack of facilities did a very good job of educating us. However, every Thursday morning we did not go directly to school; instead we went to the village church, St Bartholomew's, and a service was held which all had to participate in. For me this was not what I wanted to do and, after attending one service at which there was only me and the vicar present, I thought long and hard about what religion meant to me. I gave up being a Christian at the age of ten but not on religion.

When I was awarded a place at university, I had to apply to a hall of residence and, since most of my friends were at the YMCA, I applied there. The vicar gave me a reference and wrote about my search for meaning in life and how he wished that I would find it. At uni, I attended prayers on the first night in hall and never thereafter. I found it just as boring and meaningless as in church.

Years later, I took an interest in philosophy and started to read about the subject, much of which tended towards religious beliefs but I didn't find anything that satisfied my need. A book *Religions of the World* provided me with facts but not any great feeling that any of them were better than the others.

They say that, if you want to understand religion, then you should go to Asia. And so it was with me. I was offered a series of short secondments in the sub continent and felt that I was doing some real good there. When I had a session with a palm reader, I was dumfounded at the truths that he unveiled. In particular he told me that my religion was very personal and not based on any of the accepted faiths. How could he have known that? He also told me my age but got it one year out. When I corrected him, he insisted and then revealed that he measured from the time of conception, not birth. Whilst this produced no meaningful change in my outlook, it did somewhat reinforce the view that India was the place to discover your true self. I had dismissed Hinduism as meaningful after some explanations about the caste system and the numerous deities, who were everywhere.

I had become good friends with one of my counterparts in the City Water Department and he asked if I would visit his father in hospital. He was dying and my friend wanted me to hear what he had to say about his religion – he was a Theosophist – something I had never heard of. This opened up an interest in Eastern philosophies which were explained by the Theosophists in logical rather than faith terms. I decided to visit the headquarters of the World Theosophical Movement in Madras on my last trip there and spent some hours in the gardens where there are small chapels dedicated to the faiths of the world.

After reading more, I soon discovered that Theosophy was actually a westernised version of Hinduism, without the multiplicity of gods and castes. Of course, Hindus do not, unlike most other religions, seek converts so they are mostly people of Indian origin who have been brought up in it.

It is based on three principles which make sense to me:

You don't do good deeds because someone has prohibited all of the bad ones – you do them because you know they are the right things to do and that bad things are bad;

Your deeds and actions throughout life are accounted for and form a debt which has to be repaid in this life or the next;

Life has meaning in that each of us has something which transcends the physical world and is carried forward to another life after we pass away - some religions call it a soul, the Hindus call it 'atman'.

Dharma, Karma and Samsara are the fundamentals which most fail to see being blinded by the accoutrements which surround Hinduism.

What further convinced me to take it seriously was the commitment of Robert Oppenheimer to try and amalgamate the ancient writings of the Vedas with modern science. He called the first atomic bomb *Trinity* after the Hindu trinity of Brahma, Vishnu and Shiva – not the Christian one. Fritjof Capra wrote a book on the subject *The Tao of Physics* but failed to get to the bottom of the conundrum. The Indian Government gave a big hint when they sent a large statue of Nataraj - or Dancing Shiva to CERN which now adorns the lobby. It depicts the vacuum energy as a ring of fire which is the source of all movement in the universe and possibly the mechanism of time?

I don't seek to convert you or anyone else and I will happily discuss religion with anyone who wants to talk about it. I was brought up a Christian; I have read the Koran from beginning to end; I respect the Jews; I invite The Jehovah's Witnesses in for tea and I have prayed with the Mormons. Whilst most would not consider me religious, I have spent more time researching the subject than most people who do consider themselves religious. I accept that my views are not mainstream but they are my own and I do take exception to anyone who, however well meaning, tries forcibly to convert me to their own.

HOGGRILLS END BY PYOTR

I really must apologise for this 'story'. It was supposed to be a novel in the traditional sense but I don't suppose it's ever going to happen. To write a novel, you need a basic idea for a plot, and then you need the three essentials of story writing: a beginning; middle and an end. I suppose you could say that I have a beginning as I started writing this but that's not really enough. The real beginning to this story began fifteen years ago when I moved here and started out looking for the other five 'Station Houses' which were built by the newly created LMS in 1926 and are all identical to mine. Looking on-line (the internet not the railway) I soon found one located a few miles away and set out to find it. This turned out to be a little more difficult than expected as it was actually a mirror image and it had been painted lemon yellow rather than the standard white pebbledash with black woodwork.

Having eventually located it, I was driving back home along a minor road when I saw a small road sign which said "*Hoggrills End*". What a super name, I thought and immediately turned up the small lane which was indicated. I went over the railway bridge and meandered along a narrow lane which appeared to go nowhere. After passing some rather nice houses, I turned right at a minor junction and saw, possibly, the nicest house I have ever seen. Through the gateway, half engulfed in rhododendrons, there was a glimpse of a very old, possibly medieval or Elizabethan house which was as beautiful as any picture postcard. I fell in love with it on the spot. I couldn't stop too long outside else the owners might think I was 'casing the joint' so continued up the road. At the next crossing of paths, I found a very old thatched house with a somewhat modern extension which was under reconstruction with scaffolding over half of the façade. I was tempted to ascertain if this was for sale but, having only just moved myself, I gave up and continued my quest for Hoggrill.

Actually, Hoggrills End is neither a village nor even a hamlet, rather just a collection of narrow lanes between two 'B' roads with some very nice houses situated along it. Hardly any traffic to worry about, just the Captains of Midlands Industry on the daily commute and Madame's trip to the hairdressers or Waitrose. Over the years I have often detoured through the lanes and admired the properties, all of which are way beyond my means. In my dreams about living there I conjured up the idea of writing the novel but it's never come to pass. Let me say, at once, that I have done quite a bit of writing in my time. As an engineer in the water industry, I wrote manuals, practices, procedures and lots more, all of a technical nature and they were generally well appreciated and, in some cases, served as models for national specifications. I was also noted as an excellent writer of letters and later, in my international work, as a valued compiler of bid documents, I was never, ever, beaten on a technical bid.

I started story writing when I was working in Pakistan and had some time to spare in the evenings. I had just witnessed a group of crows attacking a young mynah bird and a lady colleague going out to rescue it. What a great beginning for a story, I thought and wrote it up. I was going to follow up with more about my female colleague as she was the exception, working on such a project at that time. Instead, I decided to follow a different train of thought and wrote about the bird instead. *The Scargill Memorial* was the result but I found the tedium of writing a full scale novel to be too much and decided to make it into a film script instead. Even this proved problematical and it soon became a 'treatment'. This tells you much about my attention span and also attention to detail. If the task becomes too onerous, and I can't see an end result, it either gets scrapped or put aside for another day. Whilst it took years to come together, I did eventually find a middle and an end to the story and it was completed though some twenty years after I first started it.

In between times I often wrote down ideas for stories but rarely, until recently, actually wrote them up in a readable form. There were some exceptions, for instance *A Job for Life* and *A Nod and a Wink*, both of which were published. So, around the time I moved here, and was working intermittently abroad, I had been introduced by my sister to opera – or rather to be more precise – Puccini. I took to it as someone who had been denied sweets during childhood but soon discovered, as in so many areas in life, that there is both good opera and bad. Probably it's more accurate to say that there are things which grab your attention and the rest – a large proportion – which a simply boring. Puccini is the exception as all of his works have good story lines and some superb arias. It was this appreciation of his arias that lead me to my next major work which I called *One Fine Day* after that haunting aria from Madame Butterfly. It tells of ex performers of the Nagasaki Opera (it was there that MB was set) having to flee in the face of war and their salvation in San Francisco. It consists of a script with many of the most popular arias and duets from classical opera with a few more modern things thrown in as linkage.

Later, I took a strong interest in particle physics and have written a number of papers on the theme of linking modern physics with the ancient Hindu writings of the Vedas. *The Dance of Shiva* is my attempt to explain where modern physics, especially the concentration on string theory, is misplaced and goes on to explain the mechanism of time. But then I forget. Long before we were all using computers to write, I had compiled a book explaining what you had to do to win at Monopoly. It was over two years after writing it by hand, before I got it typed and by that time Giles Brandreth had published *The Monopoly Omnibus*. Whilst his was inferior (IMHO) in content, it was in print and mine remains out of sight, unpublished.

So I had a beginning but no plot and idea of where to go next. My instinct was to compile a double middle section: one part dealing with Hoggrill himself and the other with my advancement in society until I found myself in a position to buy the house of my dreams in Hoggrills End. Well, actually it's a bit late to consider my place in society. I have never have been a trailblazer except in my own specialist field which was main drainage or 'sewerage' as some call it. Let me explain that 'sewerage' is not a posh way of saying 'sewage' but a collection of pipes through which 'sewage' runs on its way to the 'sewage treatment plant' and hence back into the environment. I remember one of the guys commenting "It may be shit to you but it's bread and butter to me!"

It was a good career path for me as I found out in the final year at college that I was not nearly as academic as originally thought and the endless blackboards of equations became meaningless less than half way through the year. I learned more about civil engineering in my holiday jobs with contractors Thomas Vale than I ever did in college. Half of the vacation was taken up labouring, especially making and pouring concrete and the other half with the junior engineers setting out on new contracts. Whilst labouring I had once earned £28 for a seven day week whilst my sister, one the top setters at Worth's Carpets, had brought home £24. The other half of the job paid only £8 per week but was extremely valuable experience. So much so that, my friend on the same course as me at college, who worked on the buses in Morecambe during _his_ holidays, would copy and adapt my vacation report and submit it as his experience.

I had found out at college, though it had been suspected at school, that I would seek the easy path in life and not exert myself when confronted with a choice. When going back to school for The Old Boys Dinner, I found that the unruly urchin who disrupted the dinner table when I was a monitor had been awarded a knighthood and the local doctor's son had become a distinguished professor in London. What's more though, the lad who was always near the bottom of the class had become a millionaire through buying and selling defunct companies and the one who left with a single 'O' level had made a fortune in steel stockholding. So I may have made the grade but only in a very ordinary way. It's only if I'm right about the mechanism of time, and it gets published, am I going to outshine them all with a Nobel Prize for Physics.

Of course, I could seek help from an old friend who I knew at school who became head of English at a large secondary school in the Midlands. During our time doing 'A' levels we would often discuss the things which we were studying. I remember, in particular her exasperation with the main character in *Tess of The D'Urbervilles* and I gleaned so much from her that, without ever reading the book, I was able to answer questions on it in an 'O' level exam.

I had, previously, proposed to write a short essay on the structure of short stories as many consider them to be the jokes of the literary world. But this is not altogether right. It's true that stories aimed at the male adult tend to have the standard structure where the beginning paints a scene; the middle includes some (often misleading) clues and the end contains a striking punch line. I was going to call it *The Garden Path* as that's what the story tries to do – lead you up it. However, if you consider stories which are aimed at the ladies, they tend to be quite different (more like *My Secret Garden*) and this includes many major novels. Female novellas usually feature a woman who has to choose between two men; one flashy and exciting, the other being steady and somewhat boring. After various shenanigans she will usually tame the flashy one and go off with him. The middle of the story contains all of the build up and often lays false trails.

But if I'm looking at how to write a middle, let's compare Fifty Shades of Grey and The Hunger Games. Both come in multiple episodes and contain females as main characters though Ana is, initially at least, submissive rather than dominant like Katniss. After strong beginnings the girls develop their characters with over-long and somewhat repetitive middle sections but when the end comes, quite suddenly, it's married bliss with two children – a boy and a girl! It's also quite noticeable that literature which features sex is always better when written from the female point of view. Perhaps Wilbur Smith, with his alpha males is the exception though he does not seem to be a favourite with too many women; Jilly Cooper being preferred.

And I don't have an end. Of course I could write it Jane Mansfield-Park's way which tends to skimp the beginning, have a very long tortuous middle and dump the end in an epilogue. Pity the BBC playmakers trying to make sense of this and resorting to Darcy removing his shirt to get impact! Nuneaton George has a similar approach which depends more on the elegant style of writing than the content which generally centres on some pretty boring people and how much the local vicar is paid. Compare Dicken's content and style – the complete deal.

Enough of my thesis on writing styles and let's get back to the theme of this story - I don't have an ending. Without one I would have to emulate the female short story which involves a nice lady meeting a stranger abroad and having sex with him, sometimes without even discovering his name. Or should I just finish it in a quiet way like Bathsheba in Far From the Madding Crowd – she just walks away with the boring guy after the flashy one has been killed by her other suitor. Either way, did you notice that Bathsheba and Katniss have the same surname?

I wonder, if Hoggrill was ever featured in a story, was he the flashy one or the boring one?

[PS – I'm past middle age now and don't think I will ever get to write the book - but you never know]

PYOTR AND JANA AT THE ZOO BY LEE FRAKE

Pyotr was getting near to the end of his secondments in India and decided to take a short break in a hill station in the Western Ghats. Udagamandalam or Ooty – *Queen of the Hill Stations* as it is better known is over 300 miles from Madras, thus requiring an overnight journey on an express sleeper. From the mainline station at the base of the Nilgiri Hills you can go by road or (better) take the steam-hauled, narrow gauge, rack railway. This was built by the British and opened in 1906 with small carriages hauled (or pushed) by Swiss built steam engines. It is now an integral part of the *Mountain Railways of India* World Heritage Site.

Lying close to the border between Tamil Nadu and Karnataka, Ooty is the main settlement in the Nilgiri Hills – or *Blue Mountains* in Tamil (probably on account of the eucalyptus haze). It's a favourite holiday destination in particularly for honeymooners and is close to a number of wildlife sanctuaries including an elephant reserve. It's claimed that Neville Chamberlain and his associates invented snooker here in the Ooty Club and the original table where this took place is still there. In the centre of town is a replica of Charing Cross and it bears the same name.

He bought his first class ticket for the railway and was surprised to find that he was to travel in an open carriage at the front of the train; the engine being positioned at the back. It was just over half full and he immediately noticed a young lady who positioned herself a few seats away. They set off at what appeared to be a normal speed for a narrow gauge train, leaving a cloud of black smoke behind. When they reached the first tunnel he realised why the engine was at the back of the train – the smoke was overpowering in the narrow tunnel as it had nowhere to escape. He pitied the engine driver who presumably was used to it or had some protection.

Looking ahead, he noticed that the line inclined sharply just ahead; so far the trackside indicators showed an uphill gradient of about one in a hundred but what lay ahead was much steeper. As they started up the incline which the marker showed to be 1 in 12½, the train slowed and almost stopped. There was some vibration as the rack and pinion drive was engaged and then the train moved on at a snail's-pace compared to before. There were sections when the train was under normal power (if you call pushing normal) and times when they crawled on using the rack system but either way they made steady progress until they reached Coonor Station, the halfway point. Passengers were invited to disembark whilst the steam engine was restocked with fuel and water. Tea vendors plied their wares and Pyotr partook.

On getting back onto the train he engaged the young lady in conversation and found that she was a backpacker making her way around India. She had been travelling for over two months, mostly in the north but had come south because of the wonderful Hindu temples that were all over the state of Tamil Nadu. Pyotr introduced himself and found, in return, that her name was Jana; a name he was fond of as he had, in earlier years had a very strong crush on a brunette of that name. However, Jana was a slim natural blonde and if you are thinking this story involves hanky-panky then you are doomed to disappointment. They soon found common ground in their experiences of the sub-continent and talked virtually for the rest of the journey, pausing only to admire the magnificent scenery of the Nilgiri Hills.

On arrival, they took a taxi together and Jana was dropped off at a low-cost pension in town whilst Pyotr continued to a new hotel in the hills overlooking the lake. You might think this would be idyllic but the almost new hotel had been refused permission to build up as it would spoil the view of a local politician's house and so it had been constructed into the hillside and had virtually no windows with a view. Pyotr consoled himself for the lack of outlook with reading a book of Keat's poetry which he had brought with him.

Later he took a taxi into town and picked up Jana to go to the local Chinese restaurant which had been recommended as the only decent place for westerners to eat. Whilst it was satisfactory, neither of them could actually recognise the food as 'Chinese'. Pyotr invited Jana to join him the next day as he wanted to travel to the nature reserve where you could take an elephant ride or a jeep trip to see the wild elephants. Jana agreed though somewhat reluctantly at first. He gleaned that she had recently had a bad experience with a man in her life and was reluctant to trust the opposite sex. He managed to put her mind at rest and she agreed to join him.

He picked her early in a small Maruti. He was not keen on the old Ambassadors which comprised the main taxi fleets in India and had insisted on the much newer Maruti which was an Indian-made, six seat minibus based on a Suzuki chassis. He was soon to regret his choice of vehicle. The road was a modern, smooth surfaced two-lane highway which was well designed with flowing curves which fitted into the topography admirably. However, every half kilometer or so, there was a quite fierce speed bump which aimed to prevent speeding and hence reduce the amount of road kill. It was obviously successful at this and he saw very few dead animals along their route despite the amount of wildlife in the area which included the endangered Nilgiri Hills Macaque.

The speed bumps were something you had to live with but the driver's behavior was not. In India, they drive on the left but the driver insisted on driving on the right, and each time a vehicle came from the opposite direction, he swerved to the left and continued on that path for a while before resuming in the right hand lane. But his behavior at the speed bumps needed to be experienced to be believed. He would drive slowly along the normal section of road, about 15mph, and would accelerate as he approached each bump. Whilst this may have been acceptable in an Ambassador with its soft suspension and clear headroom, it was not so with the Maruti's hard suspension and lack of headroom. After the first six or so, Pyotr told the driver to stop before the next hump and explained clearly, with much sign language that he had to drive slowly over the humps and not speed up. A slight improvement ensued but the journey continued to be just a little problematical. They arrived at the reserve and followed the signs to the animal sanctuary where they disembarked with a sigh of relief.

They discovered that there were no elephant trips that day and so went on a guided tour of the reserve where they observed a herd of wild Indian elephants. Pyotr was pleased that he had his pair of compact binoculars with him were a present for a special birthday from his wife and he shared them with Jana so that they could view as if from close up. A great experience, they both declared.

On returning, they watched the 'tame' elephants which were all shackled with a chain on one leg. They had been 'rescued' from the log hauling industry when the tree felling had been ended to save the local endangered species and create the sanctuary which was in line to become, like the railway, a World Heritage Site. They were both a little concerned at how the elephants were kept and relieved that the trips on their backs were not on that day as it was very hot and humid in the tropical afternoon sun. They consumed copious amounts of cold water to combat the heat and sheltered from the sun whenever possible.

They were shocked when one of the reserve staff ran up with news that their driver was collapsed in the car with heatstroke and was unconscious. He came back with them to the Maruti and summoned a staff member who was proficient in first aid. He pronounced that the driver needed proper attention and that they should take him to the local medical centre where a doctor was available. The staff member who had alerted them drove the car whilst the first aider cradled the driver who was listless and moaning; Pyotr and Jana sat silently in the back until they arrived at the medical centre which was, fortunately, on their route back to Ooty.

The two staff members carried the listless driver in to the surgery where he was examined immediately. The doctor gave him an injection of vitamin B and told them to get him back to Ooty as soon as possible and then take him to the hospital for a further examination. It was now getting dark and the route back involved passing through a section of the reserve which was closed during the hours of darkness. They approached the checkpoint which had two 'guards' at it who told them they could not proceed. They changed their mind when the saw the collapsed driver and allowed the car through. The rest of the journey back was uneventful as the current driver was familiar with the road and skilful in dealing with the speed humps.

As they approached Ooty the driver started to come round and, when they were met by his boss at the taxi depot, he was able to walk, talk and appeared to all intents and purposes as if nothing had happened. Pyotr profusely thanked the two staff members who had rescued them and, as they would be unable to travel back that night, gave them each a generous tip to cover their overnight stay. Another driver dropped them off at their respective hotels and as they recovered their belongings from the back seat, Pyotr noted that whilst the case was there, his binoculars were missing. Jana agreed to speak with the taxi firm the following day.

When she rang Pyotr the next morning she said that there was no news of his missing binoculars but the firm had appeared evasive and somewhat shifty. She suspected that they knew what had happened but were not willing to say anything. They said their goodbyes and, apart from exchanging a single letter, that was the last they saw of each other.

Two months later. Pyotr was in Madras again on his last secondment. None of his colleagues were in the hotel that night as he had flown out with Air India and had stopped overnight in the same hotel in Delhi as them but they were with British Airways partner Indian Airlines. Whilst Air India had spare seats and Indian Airlines were grossly overbooked for days ahead, the two airlines were forbidden to carry each other's passengers. So, one state airline flew less than half full between Delhi and Madras while the other suffered from a gross lack of seats; creating delays for transferring passengers.

As he dined alone he was aware of the conversation on the table next to his. This was occupied by a couple from the States who had a companion who they had known at home but not met for some time. Pyotr listened when he heard some familiar words and gathered that they had been to Ooty and had taken a trip to an animal sanctuary as he has some weeks before. It appeared that their driver had suffered heatstroke and they had to be ferried back to Ooty, along with the sick driver, by some locals from the reserve. After signing for his bill, he approached the couple and asked about their experience. He was interested to know whether he had rewarded the staff members enough for their trouble.

"How much did you give your gracious saviors for their trouble?" he asked.

"Well nothing actually," replied the man, "it was quite embarrassing; I couldn't give them anything as someone had stolen my wallet!"

[Footnote: if you thought that 'Pyotr and Jana' were familiar – It's quite likely. If you are of a certain age they probably taught you to read as Peter and Jane. They were replaced by Janet and John some years later and that is the pair that Terry Wogan used to talk about.]

# NO ESCAPE					JANE PETERS

She walked confidently past the streetlamp pretending not to show any sign of concern but her heart was pounding and her breathing shallow. She had to get around the corner and the feeble light from the lamp was little help. As her heels clicked on the cobles she looked ahead at the dark shadows which she had to pass through and suddenly she heard a sound from behind. As she turned to see what it was she felt a hand come round her face and stifle any sound before it could reach her lips. With that her right wrist was gripped with the assailants other hand and held up behind her. Within a second she was twisted round with her face pressed tightly up against the wall.

"Don't make a sound else I will hurt you." he said as she strained backwards to get a glimpse of his face. But that was in vain; her assailant was all in black and his features were hidden behind a mask with only his eyes and mouth uncovered. She struggled a little but soon gave way to his superior strength and stood still as he gently released the grip around her mouth.

"Keep quiet and I won't hurt you," he repeated "and anyway there's no one here to hear you." as he pulled her wrists together behind her back. She felt cold metal on her left wrist and heard the snap of a lock, then the other wrist and found herself securely handcuffed. She struggled a little and looked for a means of escape but then realised that her hands were against something hard in his trousers and her wriggling was making it harder. Then he was holding something close to her mouth. The gag was pushed against her lips and then the strap pulled tight around her head. Now she was helpless – handcuffed and gagged! She heard her attacker chuckle and then she was turned to face him. All black – nothing to see at all in the dim light from the lamp but what did it matter.

She heard the sound of his zip and realised that her was bringing out his penis but she couldn't see it. Next thing her skirt was being raised and she could feel the cool breeze around her stocking tops.

"Wow," she heard, "no panties tonight!"

With that she was restrained back against the wall and he was pushing one of his knees between hers to force her legs apart. She yielded to avoid pain and then he was firmly between her legs – she was wide open and his erect penis was touching her. She had no option but to allow him into her and, as he sank in as deep as he could, he soothed:

"How's that, my dear, just how you like it?"

With that he proceeded to screw her as hard as he could until moments later he came off with a stupendous shudder; shooting the contents of his organs into her with all of the passion he could muster. Unexpectedly she came off as he ejaculated though she was unable, gagged as she was, to utter more than a low moan to signify it.

As she came out of the ladies locker room into the reception she saw that he was already there paying the bill with his credit card.

"Have we got time for a drink on the way home?" she said, "the babysitter will be there till nine?"

[Apologies to Rupert Holmes for this one]

I AM A WIMP BY PYOTR

I listened to The Jeremy Vine Show on Radio 2 one day and heard a doctor discussing the vagus nerve which all of us have in our neck. It was not long before that I had been informed, by a sports injury specialist who was referring me for treatment on my hip, that it is this nerve that is responsible for the fainting fits which some of us suffer when, for instance, we see blood – especially our own! This condition is known as 'vasovagal syncope' – fainting due to the swelling of the vagus nerve which cuts off the blood supply to the brain.

Now if you, like me, are someone who suffers from this, it can be embarrassing as many assume that it's something to be ashamed of. It's not. It either happens to you or it doesn't but sufferers can't get away from the stigma that it's some sort of cowardice – being afraid of needles or blood. Incidentally, Doc Martin suffers from it.

I remember, when I was about eight, a visitor talking at the dinner table (we were having tomato soup and toast) about having a difficult tooth extraction which then proceeded to bleed profusely. She went on and on about it until my mother noticed that I was a pale shade of grey and getting worse by the second. They lay me down on the sofa and raised my legs until I recovered. It was years before I had tomato soup again.

At secondary school we were all required to have a BCG injection in the arm. I had missed the session when my class were done and had to go the day after on my own. The injection was simply delivered into my right upper arm and I was told to go back to my class which was in another building. As I passed through the cloakroom on the way, I suddenly came over in a cold sweat and my vision became blurry. Grey spots grew before my eyes and I had to sit down. No one was around and after I had lain down on the floor for some minutes my symptoms went away and I was able to resume.

The scenario usually unfurls like this: first there is a trigger mechanism which can be blood from a cut, an injection or just someone talking about such things; this triggers a reaction in the brain. Secondly, the brain says 'I don't like this and I'm going to block it out' and delivers this message to the vagus nerve in the neck. Then, the nerve starts to swell, blocking off the blood supply to the brain which causes faintness, sweating and partial loss of vision.

If you recognise the early symptoms, it's easy to avoid passing out completely – you simply lie down and raise your legs about the level of your head. This improves the blood supply to the brain and normal service is quickly resumed. Avoidance of risk situations is a good strategy however if, like me, you have worked abroad and need regular vaccinations you need another way of dealing with it. I always tell the practitioner that I am a '*WIMP*'. This is short for ***Will Inevitably pass out during Medical Procedures*** and usually creates some amusement. I then insist on lying down for whatever it is that I have to suffer. The alternative, for more serious and lengthy procedures, is to have your GP prescribe a single valium. With that little pill, I find that they can do whatever they like and I will not carry one jot – *WIMP* or not!

LAST MINUTES   BY PERCY VERANCE

[This is an extract from the minutes of a board meeting in the offices of the White Star Line in Liverpool around the start of WW1]

"……and can we satisfy the loss adjusters as the total cost of the claim and submit it to the auditors before the closing of the annual accounts? Mr Beresford, I'm told there is still one outstanding item. As Chief Accountant, perhaps you would explain it to the Board?"

"Thank you, Mr Chairman for the opportunity to bring this final, essential matter forward for scrutiny by the assembled members. You will recall, sirs, that there was talk that someone was rearranging the ……"

He was forcibly interrupted by the Managing Director who spoke…

"I really must scotch this stupid rumour which has gotten around. What actually happened was that one of the stewards had ascertained that there were not going to be enough life jackets to go around. Being a resourceful soul, he liberated a number of the deckchairs and tossed them overboard to act as flotation devices. However well intentioned, it was actually of little use as the sea was so cold that no one survived for more than a few minutes in the freezing water."

"Yes, sir," continued the accountant, "but that's not the issue. In order to finalise the insurance claim, we need a complete valuation of all of the assets which were lost in the disaster. Everything else is accounted for and agreed with the loss adjusters but they are refusing to sign off the deckchairs as some of them were tossed overboard and hence, being made of wood, did not sink with the ship. They are saying that, under the terms of the policy, they are not responsible for flotsam and jetsam; the chairs having being thrown overboard and hence jetsam. International law would appear to support their case."

"But what's the problem?" enjoined the MD. They only cost about ten pounds each and there can't have been more than a hundred!"

"But we don't know how many were lost and if any were picked up when the rescue vessels attended after the sinking – the auditors are asking us to justify our claim for their total write-off and I will need the Board's approval to ……………………"

[Further discussion did not reach a solution but it may be noted that many years later, around the dawn of the new century, a single deckchair with the name of the Line and of the Ship went, at auction, for just over $30,000]

DON'T LET THE CAT…….. BY FELIX SCHRODINGER

I'm sure you will have heard of me though we never will have met. That's because I don't really exist – I'm a thought experiment created by Erwin Schrodinger about a hundred years ago and ever since then scientists and even some philosophers have been arguing about whether I am alive or dead. You see, they have this particle emitter which, at some unspecified time, will emit a photon into the box in which I have been imprisoned (without food and water I may add). If the particle is emitted before someone opens the box and looks inside then it will trigger a release of poisonous gas which will kill me. However, if a photon has not yet been emitted when the box is opened then the gas will not be released and I will still be alive. The idea is that someone (an observer) has to open the box and look inside the box in order to determine whether or not a particle has been emitted and hence whether I am alive or dead! To sum up – they are saying that I am neither alive nor dead UNTIL someone looks inside the box.

What a load of tosh! Do they think that I'm stupid? If you are going to such lengths in a thought experiment then the cat that you stick in the box is going to be an intelligent one and that I am. So, once they closed the box lid, the first thing I did was to put a cork in the photon emitter which, quite obviously, negates the whole point of the experiment. And then, to be sure, I sat on the gas thing so it wouldn't work anyway. Can't say I saw the point in the first place anyway.

After sorting out the risks to my life, I set about thinking. Well, why not? If I am part of a thought experiment, then it should be perfectly all right for me to think – OK? So, having been in the box for nearly a century, I started to read up on some modern management techniques – you know – 'taking a helicopter view' and that sort of thing. And then the penny dropped – and I started 'thinking outside of the box' and hey presto here I am – outside of the box.

So, being 'out' I did a little more research to find out what had happened during my incarceration and soon found myself in a city called Copenhagen but I couldn't interpret what they were saying so it was quite Bohring. And that Werner Heisenberg in Berlin wasn't much help either – he seemed uncertain about everything! Albert was quite helpful but then he buggered off to America to see his relatives; he kept going on about how special they were and how one of them was a general!

If you have any really great ideas about where physics should be heading, or even where it has gone wrong over the last century, please keep them to yourself. No one else in the scientific community is the least bit interested in <u>your</u> theories. If they read your paper, even though it may be earth shattering, then they think it might spoil <u>their</u> chances of a Nobel Prize.

Or perhaps it might even let the cat out of the bag?

You might be wondering what I spent my time thinking about during the years of my incarceration. Well, actually I spent most of it on the philosophy of physics. You see, many so called 'physicists' are hooked on equations. As long as you can calculate what is going to happen next then you don't need to understand or even question the underlying truth. And here lies much of the problem. Whilst this approach works OK for technology (the application of scientific principles to the real world) then we can carry on regardless of the underlying faults until something happens to awaken interest in what is really going on. Let's consider some examples.

No one questions special relativity as it can be seen to ordain the relative movement of bodies with respect to each other to a great degree of accuracy, even when they are moving at great speed relative to that of light which is 'proved' to be a constant. And it is predicted to allow alteration in the passage of time as speed increases. This culminates in an example whereby a person leaves earth and travels at high relative speed before returning to find that those on Earth have experienced time differently. However, relativity tells us that there is no underlying matrix (an aether) against which this can be measured so how are we supposed to ascertain that we have actually been travelling at different speeds. Also, if light is to move at a constant speed, what is it to be measured against? Einstein tells us that gravity is actually an effect whereby matter, when in motion, takes the shortest path through 'space time' which is curved. If 'space time' is not aether, then what is it?

We have lots of good quality science programs on the television these days and they constantly remind us that the Universe is 13.7 billion years old. Why? Because we can see light from that distance and no further. Whether this changes with the introduction of new space based telescopes remains to be seen. In addition, the Universe is similar in every direction (except when we want it not to be). So, if we can see light from all directions, that is 13.7 billion years old, that would mean that we are at the centre? Otherwise, light could have been travelling for longer and hence the Universe is possibly older? Or even it didn't have a beginning at all? It may well be that Hoyle's 'steady state' comes back to haunt us.

Accepted scientific dogma (yes it is actually that) says that 'the arrow of time' is dependent upon the *Second Law of Thermodynamics* which says that everything in the universe decays into a greater state of chaos. But it doesn't and anyway, to propose that a natural phenomenon depends on a law is putting things the wrong way round. The term 'entropy' is used in order to confuse mere mortals like us cats and it is always increasing. The reason this is patently wrong is because both gravity and life cause matter to coalesce and form structures. Science has known this for centuries but continues with its absurd proposition about increasing chaos as it has no practical explanation for the concept of past and present. Text books will tell you that the Second Law continues to be correct as, overall, entropy still increases as you have to extend the boundary of the matter set that is under consideration. This, as in many other areas of physics, is simply a fudge to make the current theory fit with accepted thinking.

We're told that the theory of gravity, as displayed in General Relativity has never been disproved but then we have to invent 'dark matter' to explain why it doesn't work when trying to calculate how galaxies rotate. Would it not be better to work on the premise that something else is at work in the coalescence and rotation of matter other than simply gravity? If gravity is responsible for the nature of the planets in the Solar System – why are they all so different and why do we have an asteroid belt when it should have coalesced into a planet long ago. Time to investigate why the vacuum energy is there at all and does it have a purpose? Why did the Government of India send a large statue of a dancing Shiva (Nataraj) to CERN? Were they trying to give them a clue?

Is the Universe expanding? We have only our measurements to tell us so and, would it be more reasonable to think that the mode of measurement is more likely to be at fault?

Now if we turn to the 'standard model' we find that this is the best theory of particle physics ever mooted and it certainly is. Based on a coming together of string theory and the observed output from particle accelerators it formulates the 'particle zoo' which describes the underlying bits and pieces which make up matter and the other related particles of the world in which we live. However, it goes on to theorize two particles which have not, so far been observed. The 'graviton' is purported to be a particle which, speeding back and forth between massive objects, creates a bond which draws them together. This is nonsense. Gravity, as described above, is an effect whereby matter simply takes the shortest path in curved space or space-time, whichever you prefer.

It does not require a particle to make it work. The 'Higgs Boson' was proposed by Peter Higgs many years ago as the particle which we require to explain how the other particles acquire mass. Again we have to question the underlying thought process that makes this necessary but it's actually more interesting to look at how modern science actually works.

When politicians invest billions of dollars in a big piece of new kit, that is going to explain how the universe works or at least part of it, they want some form of guarantee that the money is well spent. So, if you build a more powerful machine that is able to boldly go where physics has not gone before, would you not expect it to find 'something', other than a split infinitive, that has not been seen before. The case that the (remains of) the new particle sat within the expected range for the Higgs is down to the large range that was specified. In addition the aspirations of the individual teams who are looking at the results of the collisions are largely centered on the Nobel Prize awards rather than on the advancement of human knowledge. It's hardly surprising that two of the four teams entered into a race to publish first rather than collaborating.

Accepted theory tells us that, when the Universe was created, equal amounts of matter and anti-matter were around but the anti-matter was destroyed, leaving only the real world matter which comprises the universe today. Is this right? Accepting that the nominal distinction between them is wholly artificial, and not wanting to discuss parallel universes, is it not more likely that both exist in equal quantities today? An anti-matter universe would emit photons in exactly the same manner as one comprised of normal matter and so it is impossible to tell the difference between the two unless they are in the process of interacting with each other. An alternative theory of creation, based on the 'steady state' would propose that each and every galaxy has a counterpart elsewhere which is made up of the mirror image matter. A possible proof would involve the discovery of two apparently identical galaxies.

I spent a little time thinking about the 'strong force', having already given my views on the 'weak force' elsewhere. Is it even a force? It is purported to hold neutrons and protons of the nucleus together but could another, simpler mechanism be the answer? If the so called particles are just the visible ends of charged strings then the thing that is holding them together would be the tensile strength of the strings rather than some esoteric gluon flitting back and forth.

In between my ruminations, for relaxation, I watched the cricket at Headingly. Being akin to meditation when Boycott was batting, I had lots of spare time to think about these issues and accept that most of this will not be your cup of (Yorkshire) tea but I exhort you to do do as they do up there –

Think On!

UNIVERSITY CHALLENGE BY PYOTR

At my university hall of residence I met Mikey; I was doing engineering and he had been sent down to Manchester by his father to learn about the textile trade. His family co-owned a famous sport shirt maker who, even then, was suffering from cheap imports from southern Asia. He was on a course which included dressmaking and he certainly got some stick about that from others in the YMCA where we lived.

When I graduated and he had left his course to work at Kellogg's, we decided to take a flat in a leafy suburb at the enormous rent of £5 a week. As a trainee under agreement, my net wage was only £11 a week so even that was a struggle and we were always a little behind. Our landlord was a kindly man, a builder by trade and a freemason. I remember his words when we met for the first time: "Can't stop long – I'm off to the Lodge for an induction tonight." Masonry, in the North of England, was not the secret society which I encountered later in life in the Midlands.

Our flat was furnished basically with a minute kitchen; we had a two bar electric fire for heating but, being on the middle floor we benefitted from heating from both above and below. Monday evenings, without fail we put the black and white telly on at eight to watch *University Challenge*. This was partially due to us both being competitive and the fact that Mikey was a dead ringer for Bamber Gascoigne.

When we went in the local chippy the lady behind the counter would exclaim "Bamber it's you again!" or some such greeting.

We played for sixpence an answer. You had to give the answer to a question clearly before anyone of those on the telly or each other and a score was kept with pencil and paper. When the programme was over the score was totted up and the debt settled. Despite Mikey's expensive education, at a public school in Scotland, I usually managed to win though narrowly and it certainly didn't make me rich.

University Challenge was abandoned by ITV some years later and we all forgot about it until the BBC took it up again under Jeremy Paxman whose acerbic wit is often trotted out when someone gives a silly answer. Mikey passed away around this time so we never got to challenge each other during the Paxman era which was, of course, in colour though the format had not changed one jot.

I still play whenever I have Monday evening free and particularly follow the fortunes of Manchester who have been successful four times to date. I still keep a rough score though I don't have to shout out the answer now that I'm watching on my own. In the early rounds, when the questions are easier, I can sometimes get around ten right though many will be intelligent guesses like "Keats" whenever there is a question on poetry and "Aristotle" for anything on philosophy.

Last week I got more right than the losing team and (would have) won five bob.

LOOK BACK IN...... BY PYOTR

It was the early 1960s and most entertainment was black and white. Whilst Hollywood produced elaborate Technicolor extravaganzas, most British films were still squarely in the monochrome era. Television plays were exclusively B&W and it was the era of the 'kitchen sink' dramas. *Room at the Top* and John Osborne's *Look Back in Anger* were very much in vogue as *Coronation Street* commenced its interminable run.

I had just finished my holiday job at the wood yard and was looking forward to going to university to study engineering when I got an urgent message from my sister to help them out. Her sister-in-law, Justine, who was a year older than me, was stopping over with them and they didn't know how to keep her entertained. I got on the bus for the hour long journey as soon as I could and arrived there later the same day. We were introduced and I was immediately taken with her looks and how sexy she was. We conversed and as we walked along the river bank, it soon came out that her parents had given up on her and wanted her brother to give her some advice. She was a striking brunette with a lovely figure and very good looks with the exception that her nose was a little on the big side. Being half French she exuded the sexiness that they, along with the Italians, tend to give out. All was well so my sister and brother-in-law were well satisfied that they had some help to keep her entertained during her stay.

After three days, during which we enjoyed each others' company she was due to depart back to the south coast. We were out walking the dog on her last day and I made a pass (what an out of date expression that is) and she responded to me kissing her. She was showing a little bare skin around her waist and I admired her black panties which appeared to be showing. "It's a suspender belt." she corrected me and looked expectantly. "Would you like to make love?" I asked and she said "Yes, but not here. What if someone comes?" So it was no go there along the river bank but she said that I should come and visit her in bed that night.

So, I crept quietly upstairs with great trepidation in case my sister and her husband should hear me – they were asleep in the next room. "So you came," she said when I gently woke her. "I thought you had given up on me."

We made love three times though she refused to use a condom and so I had to be 'careful'. In between our lovemaking which she found somewhat disappointing – apparently her Persian boyfriend's cock was twice the size of mine – she told me in some detail how they did it at least six times a night usually in a chair. I asked her if she was worried about getting pregnant as they took no precautions and she replied that she had been OK so far and was not worried. She did however ask what I would do if I got her pregnant. I replied, without commitment, that we would have to cross that bridge if we came to it. The morning after, I had a terrible sort of hangover, not being used to such 'exercise'.

Months later, I was back home when my mother opened a letter from my sister which contained the news that Justine was in a Catholic home, run by nuns, where she had given birth to a baby boy. Both were well and (as was usual in those days) the baby would go for adoption.

"She must have been pregnant when she came here," my mother said to my sister. I crept upstairs and consulted my diary. As I feared – just about nine months since we had parted. There was no further communication and I got asked no awkward questions.

About four years later, my brother-in-law's father died and, about a month after the funeral, I offered to provide transport down to the coast so that he could check that his mother was doing OK after the shock of losing her husband. We went in my beat-up car which I had bought at auction a month before.

Everything was fine and his mother had gotten over things so our trip went well. We were due to leave the morning after and Justine was there with us looking very smart. She was going out for the evening to see Georgie Fame and The Blue Flames who she knew quite well. I looked at her curiously as she seemed different and then the penny dropped; her nose, which had been quite prominent, was now a pert little job which made her look quite like Elizabeth Taylor! I started to ask what had happened and she promptly shushed me with a finger to her lips. My sister looked across and indicated that I should be quiet.

Shortly afterwards she retired to her bedroom to complete her makeup and after a few minutes, I plucked up courage and followed her. I immediately asked her about her nose and she explained that she had been in a car accident whilst in the United States and it was before we all had seat belts. Her nose had been badly broken but the insurance had paid an expensive plastic surgeon to put things right. It had been a wonderful success when healed but they had never told her mother about the car crash. Her mother had not noticed the change and they wanted it kept that way.

I then broached the subject of the baby and at once she assured me that I was not the father. I suppose it would have been easy to tell a baby of Persian descent from an Anglo-Saxon but then she was quite dark herself. Either way, the boys in my own family tend to carry our distinctive nose which turns up at the end and finishes in a cute blobby shape. I let it go as there was nothing to gain from further interrogation but I still had a lingering doubt. Years went by and I heard no more of her after she had married and settled down with a couple of children.

Increasingly I noticed programmes on the television about adopted children seeking out their biological parents and it revived memories of that summer day (night actually) just before I went up to uni.

Last year, the doorbell rang when I wasn't expecting anyone and I went to answer. A slim man in his late fifties stood there expectantly with a document folder in hand. He didn't look like he was selling double glazing.

"Pyotr….." he said inquiringly as I looked at him.

"Come in," I said to the complete stranger with the familiar face, "I've been expecting you for some time."

UNIDENTIFIED BY PYOTR

I suppose that, if I told you I had seen a UFO, you would say that I was mad, stupid or mistaken. Well I haven't so there. Actually it was an unidentified <u>aerial</u> object as it obviously was not flying at the time it was observed.

It was the early 1970s and we lived in Bury just north of Manchester. I have always been interested in aircraft as I wanted to join the RAF after school but that was not to be as I had a perforated ear drum. Anyway, I often saw commercial aircraft coming in from the north which skirted the City to the east before landing at Ringway as Manchester Airport was then called.

But today was different and I could see no commercial flights on their normal path until something caught my eye. Looking up and somewhat to the east was a very bright light in the sky. It appeared very much like Venus at night when at her brightest but this was early afternoon and broad daylight. I alerted my wife who came out to look and expressed doubt as to what it was. The neighbours were equally dumbfounded but soon lost interest and went back inside.

After about ten minutes I saw an aircraft which flew towards the house and some little distance away from the object in the sky which had not moved. I later identified it as a

Lockheed Neptune – an American naval reconnaissance aircraft. Never seen before and never seen since. Shortly afterwards an RAF interceptor flew due north and, again, a short distance from the bright object. Neither of the planes deviated and neither came back but they were not normal visitors to the local skies.

I eventually plucked up courage and called the police, not knowing who else to alert and about five minutes later a bobby in a panda car turned up enquiring where was this object in the sky?

"Right there," I told him and he looked up in astonishment.

"I see what you mean," he said and got on his radio. With that he promptly left to meet his mate in Radcliffe who had powerful binoculars which would enable him to see the object more clearly.

I watched the object for over an hour when a thin cloud came over and reduced its brightness but it remained stationary in the sky. Shortly after, it broke into three parts; the central one stayed put whilst the other two moved apart, making three in a line, and then stopped. This configuration remained static in the sky for about ten minutes and then all three faded until they could no longer be seen.

The young bobby returned shortly after, having viewed the object through binoculars. He reported that it appeared to be a bright metallic object which was revolving quite quickly and the light was reflection from the Sun. He went back to the station to report and his description of the object was reported in the local press two days later along with our names and location. This caused some annoyance as everyone who had not seen the "flying Saucer" thought we were suffering from hallucinations or some such malady.

As a result of the press report, we were contacted by a UFO organisation who requested us to fill in witness statements and return them. As I was the contact I read them all and was amazed to find that the statement of the young lad from next door, described the object just as the policeman had seen it though they had not been in contact with each other. He said it was like an ice cream cone and turning over and over.

Shortly after, I was contacted by another UFO specialist who had seen it from a location about four miles south of mine. We collaborated and with some crude triangulation concluded that the object had been at a height somewhere around five to seven thousand feet. He had not witnessed the breakup.

A week later, I got a letter from the Ministry of Defence telling me that they received many such reports each year but such things were not seen as a threat to national security.

I have never come across any reasonable explanation for what we saw that day but it certainly was not a UFO as it wasn't FLYING, however it was definitely an object and it was certainly UNIDENTIFIED.

RULES OF ENGAGEMENT   BY ADRIAN SWALL

It came about as part of the new international accord concerning the minimization of civilian casualties in conflict areas. All of the western powers were quick to sign up and ratify the agreement but no one foresaw that the Russians would also join in. All of the signatories undertook to take the necessary measures to minimize the killing or injury of non-combatants whenever they were engaged in hostilities. And, as part of the agreement, there would be an exchange of observers who were themselves experienced in combat.

So this is how I came to be seconded to my equivalent operation on the Russian side of the conflict. I soon found that they tended to rely on piloted airstrikes which was not my own specialty and I was relieved when I was placed in one of their few drone operations centres. You don't need to be anywhere near the conflict zone itself when in command of a drone though you do need to be aware of the local topography and familiar with the inhabited areas.

Like many of our own operators, we were situated in an adapted shipping container which, in this case, was located on the military base in Crimea. Most of the technology was somewhat familiar and reliable though with less reliance on modern electronics. It seemed more like being actually in the cockpit of a plane and flying the drone was very much like being in a simulator. I took my place as an overseer behind my counterpart, Yuri, and his co-pilot who was responsible for flying the drone. Yuri was in command and controlled the weapons which the drone carried – the Russian counterpart of our 'Hellfire' missiles.

We took off and Yuri relayed instructions to the pilot in order to approach the target which was in a village in the rebel area in the north of the country. The Russians provided air support in their half of the operation against the militants and the allies provided it the other half. The drone had taken off from an airfield close to the conflict zone so we were soon able to observe the target area. Yuri directed the pilot and confirmed the target. We approached from some distance to observe and confirm that the building was occupied by a number of men who were accompanied by bodyguards who lounged in the adjacent compound.

The building itself was surrounded by poorly built houses which were all occupied; children were playing in the street and a woman was hanging out washing. All this was clear to us and I expected Yuri to call a 'no go' on the operation but all he did was to confirm that he had acquired the target and that the men who they wanted were still there. I watched in disbelief as he armed the weapons pod and released the missiles which hit their target within seconds of each other.

"But what about the civilians you just killed?" I exclaimed – "your government has just undertaken to minimize casualties."

"Of course," he said "that's what we are doing."

"How can you say that when you just fired on a heavily populated area and have killed or maimed many women and children who were nothing to do with the target and probably didn't even know they were there?"

"My orders were to take out a building which, according to our intelligence, contained six of the senior commanders of the rebel force. I carried out that task and have no doubt that my operation was strictly in accordance with the undertaking of my government."

"But how can you justify the killing of those innocent civilians which you have just blown up?"

"Whilst we agree with you in principle, we have a different view of how to achieve the objective. We both agree that killing innocent people is wrong and that casualties are to be minimized, however, we maintain that the way to do this is to achieve our objectives with utmost speed and get the battle over with as soon as possible. Your way, where your planes turn back more often than not, just prolongs the conflict and, in the long run, results in more civilian deaths, more often through starvation and disease."

When I returned to my own side, I witnessed what he had been saying. Tornadoes took off and returned time and time again with their bomb loads intact. Flight controllers seemed reluctant to engage any target where there was a potential risk of harm to civilians and consequently the war ground to a halt. We were aware that the rebels used the population as a shield at times but seemed to have no means of getting round this. I was struck by the way this did not happen in the Russian sphere and now knew why – the militants knew that it was ineffective as they would be fired on regardless of any collateral damage.

I went back to my own side and cast my mind back to a conversation with Yuri just before I left him which had clarified the difference in our way of thinking. He offered me some examples.

"When you have a kidnapping, in most cases a ransom is paid; you even have a company which specializes in negotiating with kidnappers and pays up. We don't. Rebels took a whole theatre full of hostages and both rebels and many hostages died when we filled the place with poison gas. They don't do it any more as we leveled their villages when we found out who they were. Genghis Khan, Napoleon, Stalin and Hitler, are amongst many others, who realized very early on that you don't win battles by avoiding civilian casualties. If you want to minimize casualties in the long run then you don't let anything get in the way of winning as quickly as you can. Time is not only money – it's fatalities as well. You may say that this is not the British way of doing things but you would be wrong; Oliver Cromwell, Clive of India and Bomber Harris are obvious examples. Montgomery understood it but Eisenhower didn't which is why we took Berlin whilst you were still miles away and worrying about Dresden. Wellington was an exception which just goes to prove the rule. Civil liberty groups may appear to reflect the conscience of the World but they have become body counters who actually prolong conflict and hence increase casualties."

"You have suffered for years with your oil tankers being held to ransom off the coast of Africa; we don't. One of the first ships to be taken was a small tanker of ours which we used to supply customers with refined fuel when we can't supply by pipeline. After it was taken, it was anchored in a harbour and a ransom demanded. We simply bombed it and set fire to the spreading fuel oil which polluted their harbour and wiped out the local fishery for years. They don't mess with our ships anymore. They continue to take yours, despite the naval patrols, because your insurers continue to pay up. Our methods, whilst crude, are more effective in the long term."

Looking at the news, I see that there are still over 10,000 civilians trapped in our zone of conflict as the firing and bombing continues. The Russian zone has been liberated and UNICEF have set up a camp for the displaced. A task force has started clearing the roads and aid is coming in to repair or demolish the damaged structures. Life is returning to normal.

I wrote a paper for the Ministry of Defence and presented it at Chatham House last year. It did not go down well. So, if you know of anyone who requires the services of a young unemployed air force captain, with experience of drone strikes, please get in touch.

SWOOP AND SQUAT　　　　　　　BY PYOTR

Like me, you may have been unfamiliar with the term but once experienced it's never forgotten.

It was about six in the evening on a winter's day and I had been to B&Q to pick up some tiles for my bathroom so it was well after dark. I stopped at the chippy to pick up a pie and chips on my way home and must have been 'clocked' as they say when someone with bad intentions picks you out as their victim. As I set off, another car, an orange A3 pulled out some way in front and a red saloon followed me. We proceeded past the theme park and out of the 40mph zone into the 50. Some way in front I saw a white car pull out and accelerate so as not to slow us down but it was a little strange as this is a fast section of road and we were only doing forty.

We entered a short section of dual carriageway which has been marked down to a single lane as there is a junction ahead. Just before the junction there is a 'turn back' in the reservation and, completely without warning the white car which was leading suddenly braked hard and entered it. I looked to the side to see why and was suddenly confronted with the orange Audi stationary in front of me. I braked hard but could not avoid the ensuing shunt. There was the loud bang of metal and bumpers and the bonnet of my Accord bent up. My lights stayed on so I had a clear view of the Audi circles on the rear of the A3 but my glasses had fallen off onto my lap. The airbags did not deploy so the collision must have been fairly slow.

What happened next was strange: the young man in the passenger seat of the car in front jumped out and ran away. He had his arm in a sling and ran somewhat awkwardly. Then the driver came back and enquired what had happened. He was completely unfazed and polite, helping me find my glasses and then enquiring if I was OK. The driver behind had pulled up and put his hazard lights on so there was little risk of further damage. The three lads from the Audi then pushed my car to safety at the side of the road and I exchanged details with the other driver. However, he declined to give his address and his passengers were reluctant to reveal their names.

When the driver from behind said that he had called the police, they promptly left in their car which was hardly damaged. The police car arrived about ten minutes later and stayed until I had a tow back to my house, about three miles away. No one had been hurt and no statements were taken.

I informed NFU, my insurers, who were very supportive and I compiled a detailed statement the day after. However, as soon as I related my misfortune to my friends, they all, with one voice said that I had been set up. I looked on-line and soon found that my 'accident' was typical of a setup called 'swoop and squat'. Two cars are together in front of you and the leading one does something silly. The following car then stops abruptly in front of you causing a shunt. Whilst no one is hurt, the subsequent claims for whiplash and associated injuries amounts to thousands – even tens of thousands in some cases.

Having details to hand, I discovered the website of the other driver's insurers and found a broker consortium in Ireland who insure those who could not get cover elsewhere and their minimum excess was £3,000! The NFU sent a private investigator to see me and take a statement and following this they dealt with the claim.

Some time later I got a letter confirming that the other driver had had six similar incidents recorded over the previous six years and they had disputed the claim as the accident was obviously a 'manufactured incident'. They refused to pay up but did not, so far as I am aware, inform the police.

Birmingham and the surrounding area has the reputation of being the worst hotspot in the country for such scams so please be aware if you are travelling anywhere in the West Midlands.

Requiem

I held a sparrow in my hand and thought of England, lovely land

Of rocky crags and rolling downs, Black Country hags and smoky towns
But is this England we now see? It's not the one that nurtured me
Strange headdress everywhere and calls to prayer that we must share
My children say I must not care - and truth to speak, I do not dare!
But now I'm gone, I've paid my fee; spring daffodils no more to see
I miss my land, my family, but most of all miss you and me

But Shiva's call is mine to get; my soul and his will mingle yet